Underground Warrior

It was the slightest of sounds, the faint rustling of someone's clothing, maybe the sole of a shoe brushing the floor. But to Joe's keyed-up senses it sounded as if an alarm were going off right behind him.

He whirled around, his right fist ready, then lashed out as he faced a dim shape poised to jump him.

The shiver that went down his arm told him he had made solid contact with a jaw. And the figure toppling backward confirmed his observation.

At the same time, Frank had swivelled around to find a blunt instrument being thrust down at him. He grabbed the wrist of the hand holding the weapon, flipped the man it belonged to, and without breaking his flow of movement, delivered a knock-out chop to the back of the man's neck.

Then, blackness. Blackness filled with pain, as hard rubber truncheons were hammered down on their skulls. . . .

D1392783

Other Hardy Boys Casefiles™ available in Armada

THE HARDY BOYS CASEFILES™

Casefile 5
Edge of Destruction

Franklin W. Dixon

ARMADA

First published in the USA in 1987 by
Simon & Schuster, Inc.
First published in Great Britain
in Armada in 1989

Armada is an imprint of
the Children's Division, part of
the Collins Publishing Group,
8 Grafton Street, London W1X 3LA

Printed and bound in Great Britain by
William Collins Sons & Co. Ltd, Glasgow

Edge of Destruction

Chapter
1

"JOE! WATCH IT!" Frank Hardy grabbed his younger brother's arm. He yanked Joe from the path of a guy in a tuxedo who was charging for the ballroom exit.

Until a few minutes before, the wealthy and famous had jammed the mid-Manhattan hotel ballroom for a political gathering. But as the room slowly filled with smoke, the distinguished group was being turned into a panic-stricken mob.

The purpose of the gathering had been to kick off the mayoral campaign of Chief of Police Samuel Peterson. Right then, though, Peterson's supporters were busy running for exits. Peterson himself remained cool and stood in front of a microphone, trying to calm the crowd. "Don't panic. Exit in an orderly fashion," he instructed.

1

He might as well have been talking to himself. As the smoke grew thicker, his voice was drowned out by shouts, screams, curses, and waves of choking sounds.

"The doors are locked! We're trapped!" a man yelled, his shrieks dissolving into a series of wracking coughs. Soon the guests were fighting to get out.

The smoke had become so dense that Joe and Frank Hardy, standing side by side, could barely see each other. Frank grabbed a napkin from one of the tables and held it over his face.

"What do we do?" Joe shouted into his brother's ear. Joe knew he couldn't charge into action. Too many people around him were doing that, and they were only adding to the chaos.

"Keep cool!" Frank shouted back. But when he tried to figure out how to calm the fear-crazed crowd, he came up with zero. He was ready to admit defeat, all set to tell Joe it was every man for himself. Then he saw he didn't have to.

"Hey, the smoke's not that thick anymore," he said. "I can even feel the air-conditioning again."

Joe nodded. "Somebody must have put out the fire."

All around them, other people were making the same discovery. The shouting and screaming turned into a buzz as the smoke thinned. The guests were looking slightly sheepish.

Samuel Peterson's voice could be heard clearly over the microphone then. "The trouble seems to be over now," he said. "As soon as we find out exactly what has happened, we'll make an announcement."

A man angrily waved his fist and shouted, "But we're still locked in! What's going on?" As if in answer, the doors to the ballroom were smashed open, and police came pouring into the room.

"Peterson must have called them," said Frank. "I understand he's in constant radio contact with his men."

Peterson talked with an officer for a minute, then turned back to the microphone. "We still don't know what caused the smoke," he reported. "But no fire's been found. So let's act like New Yorkers and not let this incident throw us." Then, raising his arms enthusiastically, Peterson shouted, "Okay now, everybody, let's get on with the party!"

His words were greeted with applause. Then the band members, who had returned to their places, played a smooth rendition of "Smoke Gets in Your Eyes."

"Nice choice," said Frank.

"I'd rather hear some Stones," said Joe, not getting the joke. He looked at the guests. "But these people would probably think it was too loud. They look—old."

"Old—and rich. Like Dad told us, most of this crowd has been invited so they'll give big bucks for Peterson's race this fall," Frank said, looking at the formally dressed guests.

The Hardy boys were wearing suits and ties for the first time that summer. "You have to," their father, Fenton Hardy, had told them when they protested. "That is, if you want to meet Peterson." The boys wanted to meet Peterson, so they wore ties. And Joe complained the whole time that his was strangling him.

For years they had heard about the police chief from their father, who often reminisced about when he had worked as a New York City police detective. That was before he'd set out on his own as a private investigator. Peterson had been Mr. Hardy's partner on the force. The Peterson-Hardy combination had cracked some of the toughest cases in the department's history.

Sam Peterson had also cracked some long-standing traditions. As the leader of the Guardians, the black police officers' association, Peterson had demonstrated the skills and smarts that eventually got him appointed chief. The two men had kept in touch, and Hardy was one of the first people Peterson had told about his decision to run for mayor.

"He's invited me to come to his campaign opener," Fenton Hardy had told Frank and Joe. "And he said to bring the two of you along. I've told him a lot about you—like any parent, I can't resist bragging a little about my kids. Anyway, he wants to meet you."

"And I'd like to meet him," said Frank enthusiastically. "From what you've told us about him,

4

he'll make quite a mayor if he manages to get elected."

"Yeah, and I bet he will be," said Joe. "He's my kind of guy."

"If you go with me, you have to be prepared to mingle with an older crowd," warned Mr. Hardy. "Big-city politics isn't kid stuff."

"That's okay. We'll do anything." Joe grinned. "If you want us to, we can dye our hair white at the temples."

"And put a little stuffing around our waists." Frank grinned, too, looking pointedly at his father's stomach bulging slightly above his belt.

Fenton Hardy gave his belly an affectionate pat. "I've got to lay off those chocolate-chip cookies and put in a few more hours at the tennis club." He smiled ruefully. "I'll appoint you my guardians at this affair—don't let me get near the buffet."

Now, standing in the ballroom, Frank said, "Speaking of Dad, let's find out what *he* thinks caused the smoke."

"I wonder where he is," said Joe, scanning the room. "Last I saw of him, he was talking to Guido Scalpia."

"Let's go ask Guido, then," said Frank. "It'll give us a chance to meet him."

When they finally met and asked the tall, distinguished-looking former Yankee center fielder about their father, he shook his head. "I was talking to him, you know, remembering when he helped catch a crank who was sending me threatening letters. But at the first whiff of smoke coming into the room, your dad went to find out what was going on. You know that all he needs is a scent of mystery and he's off and running. I've always thought he's part bloodhound."

"You're right about that. But which direction did he head in?" Frank asked.

"I don't know. Maybe he went outside to help the cops," Guido said.

Joe headed for the door, calling over his shoulder to his brother, "Let's find out." Outside the ballroom, the two brothers still had no luck. The lobby was swarming with fire fighters and cops, but none of them had seen Fenton Hardy. Most of them did know what he looked like, though.

"Maybe Peterson can help," said Frank. "It figures Dad must have gone to him when the trouble started."

They returned to the ballroom and joined the crowd around Peterson. "Hey, kids, where's your dad?" he called before they could ask. "I have some people I want him to meet."

"Beats us," said Frank. He was beginning to have a slightly uneasy feeling.

"What's Dad up to?" Joe said, almost to himself. But his thoughts were interrupted by a piercing noise coming from Peterson's breast pocket.

"A cop is never off duty," the chief said, faking a sigh. Pulling his beeper out, he flicked on the incoming-call switch.

The voice that came over the beeper was high-pitched—obviously a man trying to mask his identity.

"Hi, chiefy," the voice said, chirping cheerfully. "Don't bother hunting for your pal Fenton Hardy. No way you're going to find him. And unless you do what I say, you'll find him in a way you won't like." The voice paused for the space of a heartbeat, then went on, sounding exultantly happy. "You'll find Fenton Hardy dead, baby. Did you hear me? Dead. Dead, dead, dead, *dead*."

Chapter

2

SAMUEL PETERSON'S FACE turned hard as he listened to the voice from his beeper. He pressed the talk button. "Who are you?" he demanded. "What have you done with Fenton?"

"Come on, Chief, you really don't expect me to answer those questions," the voice said. "There's just one question you should be asking."

"What's that?" said Peterson.

" 'What do I have to do if I want to see Fenton Hardy alive again?' " the voice said.

"Okay, what *do* I do?" said Peterson. He was trying to keep his voice neutral so it gave no hint of the rage that was building up inside him.

"Right now, you do *nothing*. You just wait for me to contact you again. Oh yeah, one other thing. Keep all this to yourself. Believe me, you don't want to alert the public. Because if you do, it'll lead to a panic in the city that'll make what happened in your smoke-filled room look like a calm demonstration."

"A panic?" Peterson's voice sounded hoarse. "What do you mean? I don't get the connection."

"You will, Peterson baby, you will. For the moment, trust me," the voice continued, "and keep your trap shut tight."

Peterson's eyes were slits of fury. "Okay, you have my word. But when are you going to call again?" A clicking sound and then a buzz of static were all that answered him. The connection had been broken.

Peterson turned to Frank and Joe. "You kids heard what this joker said, right?" They nodded. "I'm sorry about your dad—really sorry. But you know to keep your mouths shut about it, right?" The chief took a deep breath, shaking his head. "Good thing you two were the only ones within earshot. It'll make security easier."

"We'll sit tight until we find out what the kidnappers want," Joe said. "Then we can make our move."

Peterson gave the Hardy boys a tolerant smile. "Look, kids, I know you want to help your father, but I suggest you leave this matter to the police. It's a job for professionals."

"We're not exactly amateurs," said Joe indignantly. He was about to tell Peterson about some of the cases he and Frank had cracked, but Frank cut him off.

"We won't get in your way," Frank assured Peterson. "But since he is our father, will you at least keep us posted on what's going on? We can't pretend we're not worried."

"Okay," said Peterson. "Keep quiet about this for the time being, and I'll let you in on what's going down."

"Thanks a lot," said Frank politely.

"Yeah, thanks a million," Joe said sarcastically.

"Maybe we'll call our mom now," Frank said before Joe could get started. "We'll tell her we're staying in the city. That way she won't get suspicious about Dad not coming home, and we'll be on hand here if anything comes up."

"You do that," said Peterson. "I'm heading back to my office, as soon as I can get away from here. Meet me at my car. It's out in front."

"See you there," said Frank. "And soon," Joe added, as the two boys headed off in search of a pay phone. "Okay, why are you giving in to Peterson?" Joe demanded as soon as they were out of sight. "He treated us like a couple of five-year-olds."

"Look, as far as Peterson is concerned, we're not much better than five-year-olds. A couple of guys still in high school don't rate in his book. He's not about to make us his partners in this case—especially since he's running for mayor.

Imagine what the headlines would say if the papers found out: 'Top Cop Turns to Kiddie Corps for Help.' The smart thing for us to do is play dumb. That'll keep Peterson happy until we get enough info to do something on our own."

Joe thought a second, then shrugged. "You know, I hate to admit it, but you're probably right." Frank gave him a grin. "But I want one thing understood," Joe went on. "Once we do get any kind of lead, we don't wait for Peterson's okay. We swing into action."

"Agreed," said Frank. Even if this case hadn't involved their dad's safety, Frank would have been hooked. He could never resist an intriguing mystery.

From a pay phone in the hotel lobby, Frank called home to Bayport. "Your mother is out at a Bayport beautification meeting," their aunt Gertrude said after answering the phone. Then she added in a worried voice, "I hope nothing's the matter."

Frank tried to laugh off his aunt's worry. "Hey, nothing's wrong. Really. I just called to say that the police chief has invited Dad, Joe, and me to stay in the city for a few days. Dad will be giving a lecture at the police academy, and Joe and I are going to get a chance to see how a big-city police department works from the inside."

"I'll tell your mother," their aunt Gertrude said. "But, Frank, dear—all of you—do be careful. I remember the last time I was in New York—"

"I know," Frank cut in. "I promise we'll be careful."

"I'm sure *you* will be," she said. "But keep an eye on Joe. He can be so impulsive."

"I'll do that," said Frank as he looked up to see Peterson and several uniformed policemen walking out of the hotel. "I have to hang up now," Frank said quickly. "Dad's signaling that we're moving on to the police chief's office."

"That's what I mean about New York," said his aunt Gertrude. "Rush, rush, rush."

"Right—and that's what I have to do. 'Bye," said Frank, hanging up. He headed after Joe, who was following Peterson out of the hotel.

Back in his office, Peterson loosened his tie and sat down behind his desk. Then he motioned for Frank and Joe to take seats facing him.

Joe tapped his fingers on the arm of his chair. "Well," he finally burst out, "what do we do now?"

"We do what we were told," said Peterson. "We wait."

They didn't have to wait long. Five minutes of tense silence later, the buzzer on Peterson's intercom sounded.

"What is it?" Peterson asked.

"Someone sent you a package," a cop said.

"Bring it up right away."

"What about security?"

Peterson thought a moment. "All right. Have it checked out. But make it a rush job."

Peterson turned from his intercom and explained. "It's routine procedure for our bomb squad to check out all incoming packages."

"Terrorists?" Frank asked.

"The threat's there all the time," said Peterson.

"You think Dad's kidnappers are terrorists?" Joe asked, his voice rising. Just the word *terrorist* was enough to make his blood boil. Not long before, the girl he had loved, Iola Morton, had fallen victim to a terrorist firebomb. Ever since, Joe had been consumed by a passion for vengeance on terrorists. And now he had to bite his lower lip to keep the rage inside him from bursting out.

"No use guessing," said Peterson. "I have a hunch that this package will give us an idea."

The package was already open when the uniformed policeman brought it in and placed it on Peterson's desk. Reaching inside, the police chief pulled out a cassette.

"It's a videotape," said Frank. "Where can we play it?"

"I've got a VCR right here in my office. It's in this cabinet." He walked to the other side of the room and opened a door of the walnut wall unit.

He turned back and noticed Frank looking at

the tape curiously. "What's the matter? Something wrong with this?" asked Peterson, holding up the tape.

"Probably not," said Frank. "I've just never seen that brand before. It's some kind of import."

The chief inserted the cassette into the VCR. The picture quality was extremely good, far above average.

An image of Joe and Frank's father appeared on the screen, absolutely clear, every detail sharp, the color lifelike.

Lifelike, though, was the wrong word, because Fenton Hardy was lying with his eyes closed and his arms folded over his chest.

His resting place was the red plush interior of a gleaming wooden coffin.

"Those pigs were lying to me," Peterson snarled. He slammed his fist against the wall. "They were keeping me off their trail, stalling for time until they could get away clean. They've already killed him!"

Chapter

3

THE THREE STARED in horror at the image of Fenton Hardy's corpse.

"Dead," said Frank in a stunned voice.

"I can't believe it," said Joe, barely able to choke out the words.

There was nothing to say, nothing to do. Silently, Peterson and the boys sat alone with their shock and grief. They glued their attention to the picture on the screen, as if by looking at it hard enough they could change what they saw.

Suddenly Frank leaped up from his chair and pointed. "Look!" Moving slowly onto the screen was the back of a hand. The hand was curled around something and covered Fenton Hardy's nose and mouth for a minute. Then it turned to display what it was holding.

"What—?" Joe looked puzzled. "A mirror?"

"Yes," Frank said excitedly. "But that's not what's important. Look what's on the mirror."

Joe looked more closely. "The center is fogged over—some kind of steam."

Frank shook his head. "That's not steam—it's condensation caused by breath on the glass." He hesitated. "Dad's breath."

"Then he's alive." Joe went limp with relief.

"Well, they picked a fine way to tell us that," Peterson said sharply as the screen went dark.

"Maybe they were trying to tell us something else, too," said Frank.

"They've told me enough," said Joe. "We have to get after them—fast."

"Relax, Joe." Peterson looked tired. "Believe me, the department is beginning to move on this. We'll be quietly checking over the whole hotel. That way, we'll find out how your dad was taken out of the place. Then, once we've picked up the trail, we'll follow it and close in. I know you're impatient to find your dad. But trust us. We have our procedures."

Joe's grimace made it clear what he thought of the ponderous police pace. "Don't forget our agreement," Peterson said, cautioning him. "I don't want you and your brother getting mixed up in all this."

"Right, right," muttered Joe, without even trying to sound as if he meant it.

Before Peterson could make his point again, the phone rang, and he picked it up. He pressed a button that let the caller's voice be projected into the room.

"I hope you enjoyed the TV show," the same high-pitched voice that had announced the kidnapping said.

"What have you done to Fenton Hardy?" Peterson demanded. "Drugged him? Beaten him unconscious?"

"What we've done is far more interesting than *that*," said the voice. "The illustrious investigator has the honor of being the first human guinea pig for a powerful new virus we've developed."

"Virus?" the chief echoed.

"That's right, chiefy. Virus Strain A—intended to leave its victims totally unconscious, but alive." A hoarse laugh grated through the speaker. "And you'll be happy to know it works. It works *perfectly*. Fenton Hardy will stay just the way you saw him until we stop feeding him through IVs or cure him with a special antibody we've created. So," the voice said after a slight pause, "are you convinced?"

"Convinced of what?" Peterson was keeping his voice calm and level, but the effort was showing.

"That we have the scientific capability of carrying out our threat. You know, for a guy that's running for mayor, you're not so smart."

Peterson ignored the slur. "I have no definite proof, but I'll have to believe you. Now may I ask, what threat?"

"Well," the voice said, "Virus Strain A isn't our only weapon. We also have Virus Strain B. So far we've used it only on laboratory animals, but it kills those little rats amazingly quickly— *after* several minutes of excruciating agony, that is."

There was a silence. Then the voice said, "What? No more questions? I thought for sure you would jump in with the one you should be *dying* to ask."

"Which is?"

"What do we plan to do with Virus B?" said the voice gleefully.

Peterson took a long, deep breath. "Okay, what *are* you planning to do?"

"We're going to release Virus B in six of New York's largest buildings. There'll be at least fifty thousand dead—and that'll be just the beginning. The entire city will go crazy with fear. New York will turn into a madhouse—and then into a ghost town."

"You're the one who's crazy, if you expect me to believe that," said Peterson.

"You've seen what we've done to Fenton Hardy. And you said you believe us. And you also witnessed what we were able to do at your gathering this evening. It will be just as easy to fill buildings with our virus as it was to fill that room in the hotel with smoke."

"Let's say for the sake of argument that you *can* do it," said Peterson. "Why *would* you?"

"Once again you're not asking the right question," the voice said sharply. "The only question that should concern you is why we *wouldn't* do it."

"Okay, why *wouldn't* you?"

"We won't do it if we receive twenty million dollars in used fifty- and hundred-dollar bills."

Peterson was poker-faced as he answered, "How do you expect me to come up with that kind of money?"

"This city is filled with banks, big businesses, millionaires, and tax collectors, Mr. Police Chief. I'm sure if you explain to certain people what they will lose if the money isn't paid, they'll decide that the price is cheap."

"But all that will take time."

"We're willing to be reasonable," said the voice. "We'll give you three days to get the money together. After you've done that, we'll tell you how to deliver it."

"Three days! That's not—"

"Actually," said the voice, "if you don't get it in two days, we'll help you speed up the collection process."

"What do you mean?"

"Believe me, you don't want to find out. Oh,

yes," the voice went on, "one more thing. Don't try to use the time we're giving you to hunt us down. The moment we spot a single cop, Fenton Hardy dies."

"But—"

"But nothing," said the voice. "Just goodbye."

"Not so fast," said Peterson. "I want—" Then he realized he was speaking into a dead line, and his expression tensed. "I was hoping to keep him on longer," he told Joe and Frank. "But I guess he talked long enough."

Frank understood immediately. "You've got a tracer on your phone. That's it, isn't it?"

"Sharp thinking," the chief said. "The tracer is part of a computerized system. As soon as I heard the kidnapper's voice, I pressed this button here. The call was instantly traced, and the nearest patrol cars were sent to the address. We should be getting news of the capture any minute now. I can't wait to see the look on your dad's face when he learns how fast we've rescued him. That should show him how far we've come since he left the force."

The phone rang. Smiling, Peterson picked up the receiver.

"Well?" he said expectantly. "You have him?" His smile vanished. "That's impossible," he said. "Check it out. And if you can't come up with anything, check it out again." Peterson slammed down the receiver.

"These so-called technical experts can't do

anything right!" he exploded. Then he got control of himself. "It's the tracer system," he said in a cold, even voice. "It doesn't work."

"What's the trouble?" Frank asked anxiously. "They couldn't trace the call?"

"They traced it, all right," said Peterson. "But the computer readout said the call had been made from a spot in the middle of Lexington Avenue, between Forty-second and Forty-third streets."

Joe slumped in his chair, as his brother sat up. "Maybe the call was made from a car phone," Frank suggested.

"Not a chance," Peterson came back. "The person making the call didn't move one inch. And not even a city traffic jam would result in a car's sitting in one place that long—at least, not without our knowing about it."

"Then what's going on?" Joe wondered.

"A snafu," said Peterson bitterly. "We're back where we were before we started. Square zero." He paused, and when he spoke again his voice was hoarse. "Actually, we're worse off. We can't make a move without putting your dad's life on the line. You can bet that from now on those scum will be watching for any sign of our coming after them. So for the time being, we're paralyzed."

Frank suddenly got to his feet, his abruptness startling not only Peterson but Joe as well. "Well," he said, "if we can't do anything but wait, there's no sense in our hanging around. We might as well head back to Bayport. At least that way we'll be able to make excuses for Dad's absence if it lasts more than a few days."

"But we can't leave the city," Joe protested.

"I'm sorry, but Frank's right," Peterson said. "There's nothing you kids can do here."

"That's what *you* say," said Joe, his temper flaring.

"Come on," Frank said, pulling at him. "You know, it's really a drag always having to keep cool for both of us."

"What's really a drag is you playing Mr. Goody Goody all the time," Joe answered, the expression in his eyes furious.

"Look," Peterson said, trying to keep the impatience out of his voice, "I know how upset you must be, but I don't have time to waste listening to your squabbles. I've got things to do, people to contact."

"What do you mean, 'people to contact'?" Joe snapped. "I thought we were paralyzed."

"I'll be talking to people about raising the ransom," Peterson said. "I don't intend to pay those scum"—his eyes went down—"but I don't want to let your father—or the city—down, either."

Frank nodded. He tugged at Joe's arm. "We might as well get out of here and let Chief Peterson do what he has to."

Joe's first reaction was to shake Frank off, but then he caught the message in his brother's eyes.

"Okay, big brother, don't push too far," Joe said, angry for Peterson's benefit. "I'm coming. We'll settle this outside."

Peterson shook hands with both boys. Then he put an arm around each of them as they walked to the door. "Remember, Frank," he said, "keep your head—and make sure your brother hangs on to his."

"I'll do my best," Frank promised convincingly.

"All right, what's up?" Joe demanded as soon as they were out of Peterson's office. "I could see from that look you gave me that something's going on in that busy brain of yours.

"We need a good night's sleep," Frank said. "We're going to a hotel, and tomorrow we're going into action!"

Chapter

4

OUTSIDE IN THE morning Joe had only one question. "Where to?" He felt too tired to say more than that. He had spent an awful night, twisting and turning. Every time he closed his eyes, he saw his father lying in that coffin, barely breathing.

Frank, too, hadn't slept well. He had had nightmares about searching for his father through scenes of plague and desolation. New Yorkers were struggling like rats in traps, spreading the deadly virus until the whole city was exterminated. He blinked his eyes and finally answered his brother's question. "Grand Central Station."

"Great," Joe complained, looking at the crowded sidewalks. "We'll never get there."

"If we don't crack this case, there won't be

anyone in the streets," Frank muttered, pulling his brother into a subway entrance. "The police can't make a move without putting Dad in deadly danger—so it's up to us to track down the kidnappers."

"Call them terrorists—because that's what they are," said Joe, his fists clenched.

"Whatever you call them, they won't be on the lookout for us," said Frank quietly, and he ran to buy two tokens. "That's why I didn't tell Peterson about the lead I thought of. He might have been tempted to send cops out to follow it up," he said after he and Joe were on the train.

"Brilliant observation, Sherlock," said Joe. "But tell me one other thing. What's this lead of yours? Or do you want to keep me in the dark too?"

"I'm surprised you didn't spot it right away," Frank said in the maddening manner he sometimes had.

"I was too busy seeing red. Frank, just thinking about those terrorists made me—"

"You know," Frank broke in, "if you saw less red, you might see more clues."

"Look," Joe snapped, "forget the big-brother lecture and just give me the lowdown."

"Always so impatient." Frank sighed. "But, if you insist—it was the videotape, Mr. Detective. A weird off-brand—Kajimaki Industries, it said. There can't be many stores that carry it, and maybe we can find out if a clerk remembers anyone buying some recently. The brand's unusual enough so that it might stick in someone's mind. The lead's worth checking, anyway—seeing as we have nothing else to go on."

"So where are we heading now?" asked Joe.

"There's a hole-in-the-wall computer store near Grand Central," said Frank, who was a dedicated PC buff. "I've bought hard-to-get computer parts there, and I've noticed the place carries a lot of cheap foreign videotapes. If nothing else, we can ask them the names of other stores to look in."

"Hmm," Joe grunted grudgingly. "Once in a while you do come up with an okay idea."

"Let's hope this one pans out," said Frank. "As Peterson said, otherwise it's back to square zero."

Joe looked out the window. "Well, here's where we find out," he said as the train came to a grinding halt at the Grand Central Station stop.

The boys joined the flow of passengers moving rapidly out of the car. In a minute they found a sign telling them which ramp to take to the surface.

"What a maze down here," said Joe. "Makes me feel like a mouse in a laboratory experiment." He looked around at all the people jostling past. It was as if everyone was in a race to be the first up the ramp. "One mouse in a mob of mice."

"The subways are just part of the underground," said Frank. "There are the railroad lines here, too. Plus a lot of other facilities. I once read a newspaper article on Grand Central Station. It said that so many different things have been built under the station since it first went up that nobody has a complete map of them all."

"Who would want one?" said Joe as they reached the top of the ramp. "Give me life above-ground anytime."

Joe didn't feel much better, though, after they made their way through the crowded station and exited up on the street.

"I still feel like I'm underground," he said. They were on a sidewalk that lay in the permanent shadow of towering buildings. Only a narrow strip of bright blue sky above them proved that it was still broad daylight. Edging the blue were dark gray clouds that would bring rain later.

Frank put his hand on Joe's arm. "Wait," he said. "Here's the store."

On the window was a big sign proclaiming SUPER SALE! GOING OUT for BUSINESS! with the word *for* written in nearly invisible ink. Inside were display counters jammed with every conceivable kind of electronic goods.

"Kajimaki videotape?" said the salesman. "You're in luck. We're the only place in town that carries it. The company went out of business last year, and we snapped up their last shipment. That's why we're able to offer it at an unbelievably low price. In fact, if you buy one of our new

VCRs, also on special sale, we'll toss in five tapes free."

"Actually, we just want some information," said Frank.

The eager gleam in the salesman's eyes faded. "You want information?" he said. "There's a big booth inside Grand Central Station that'll give you information. They'll even give it for free. This place is a *store*. We *sell* things. You give us money, we give you merchandise. Got it?"

Frank and Joe exchanged glances. This man was so warm—so friendly.

"Look, I'd like to buy some of those videotapes," Frank began. "In fact, if the price is right, maybe I'll buy you out. But first I want to be sure the stuff is okay," he said. "You ever get any complaints?"

"Absolutely not," said the salesman indignantly. "Do you think this establishment would sell anything not backed up with an iron-clad guarantee?"

"Is that your guarantee?" Frank asked, pointing. A small, faded sign was attached to the wall with peeling Scotch tape. In tiny letters, the sign said, "All sales final. Absolutely no refunds."

"Oh, *that*," said the salesman. "That's just to discourage cranks."

That got a smile from Frank. "Well," he said, "not that I don't believe you, but maybe you can tell me if you've sold many of these tapes."

31

"Sold many? Of course we have," said the salesman.

"How many?" asked Frank.

"A lot," said the salesman.

"How many is a lot?" asked Frank.

"Quite a few," said the salesman.

"How many is quite a few?" asked Frank.

"A number," said the salesman.

"What number?" asked Frank.

"Just yesterday a guy came in and bought a couple of tapes," the salesman said.

"Just one person has bought Kajimaki tape?"

"For pete's sake, kid, we just got the shipment in a couple of days ago. Kajimaki doesn't have brand recognition."

"So why did this guy buy it?" asked Frank.

"To tell the truth, he didn't actually *buy* it. I offered to toss it in free when he was trying to decide if he wanted to buy a video camera—also on special sale, incidentally. Maybe you'd like to take a look at one. I'll make you a deal you won't believe."

Frank pretended to consider. He looked at Joe, as if asking an opinion. Joe shrugged. "I'm not so sure," he said. "You think we can trust this guy?"

Frank turned back to the salesman. "Look, don't worry about my friend here. It's not that I don't trust you, but maybe you could tell me who this other person was who bought the tape. Maybe you even have his name on a credit card receipt. That way I could get in touch with him. I could check out if he's happy with it."

"No luck," the salesman said. "The guy paid in cash for the whole thing. Some people do it that way. Crisp hundred-dollar bills. I don't ask where they get them."

"Actually, I buy things the same way," said Frank. "In fact, most of my crowd does." He knew he had to try to squeeze out the last bit of information fast, before the salesman began to get suspicious. "Actually, this guy might be somebody I know. A real big spender—a video freak, too. He told me he was going to buy some new equipment. Was he a tall, skinny guy with red hair?"

"No," said the salesman. "This guy was tall, all right, but he must have weighed three hundred pounds. Plus, he was bald and had a black beard. A little weird looking, you might say, but easy to remember."

"Guess it wasn't Tim," said Frank, quickly mentioning a name. "Too bad there's no way I could find out who he is—or be able to contact him. Look, if he ever comes in again, maybe you could get more information about him and call me. I can give you a phone number."

"Yeah, right," said the salesman, his interest fading as his hopes for a sale dimmed. Then suddenly his eyes brightened. "Hey, what a break!"

Frank and Joe wheeled around to see where he

was looking. Filling the doorway was the mountain of a man that the salesman had just described.

Before they could make a move, the salesman was out from behind his counter and past them to greet the customer.

"Hello, sir!" he said. "Glad to see you again. Hope you were happy with that great Kajimaki tape you got. As a matter of fact, these two young men are interested in buying some. Maybe you could tell them—"

He didn't get to finish his sentence. The big, bald, bearded man pivoted instantly and vanished from the doorway.

The salesman turned toward the Hardy boys. "Hey," he said, "I'm sorry. I don't know what got into—"

But he didn't get to finish that sentence either. Frank and Joe tore past him, desperate to get to the sidewalk before the big man disappeared down the street.

"Hey, wait!" the salesman shouted after them from the store doorway. "I'll give you a deal you can't—" But by that time they were almost out of hearing range. They had spotted the big man racing into Grand Central Station and were running after him, weaving through swarms of pedestrians who constantly held them back. But they did manage to make it into the station shopping arcade just in time to see the man going down a flight of marble stairs.

"Let's go!" Joe said, leading the way.

At the top of the stairs, Frank saw a sign: To Trains.

"Quick," he said to Joe, who needed no urging. "He's going to leave town."

When they reached the next level down, they saw the man darting into the farthest entranceway in a line of tunnels that led to the different train platforms.

"Let's hope his train isn't pulling away right now," said Joe as they ran after him.

They got to the entrance, dashed through, and saw—nothing. There was no train on either of the tracks. In front of them, under dim electric light, the long concrete platform stretched empty into the distance.

Joe clenched his teeth angrily. "He got away!"

"But where?" said Frank. "I don't see any way out of here other than the entrance we just came through. And he couldn't have vanished into thin air. Let's check the tracks. Maybe he's crouched down there, hiding."

Joe took one side of the platform, Frank took the other. They moved cautiously, ready to spring into action. Every second or two, they glanced across the platform at each other in case one of them suddenly needed help.

"Nothing," said Joe disgustedly when they reached the end. "So, what now?"

Frank thought a minute. "Maybe, just maybe," he said, "the creep escaped down the tracks."

"Pretty slim possibility," said Joe. "But it's worth checking out"—he made a face—"considering we have no other choice."

"You go down the left track, I'll go down the right," said Frank. "We'll both give it five minutes before we come back and meet on the platform. Unless, of course, something turns up sooner. Then whoever makes the find will give a yell and hope the other hears it."

"Let's go," said Joe impatiently.

"Hold on. First we check the time and synchronize our watches."

Joe rolled his eyes. "You find more ways to waste time," he complained. But he went through the routine.

Once down on the track, Joe went all out to make up for lost time.

"If the guy did go down these tracks," he muttered to himself, "he has a big head start." Joe race-walked between the tracks, carefully avoiding the electrified rail or tripping over the ties. The light from the platform soon faded, and he turned on the combination pen and flashlight he always carried with him. Good thing Frank has one just like it, he thought. And he squinted to see what the faint glow would reveal.

Nothing.

Then he saw something in the grime that covered the track bed. Something that might be the trace of a footprint. Maybe he should go back and tell Frank, or yell for him. But going back would let the guy get away for sure. And yelling would alert him to move faster. There was a good chance the guy had slowed down, thinking he was safe.

Joe knew that by moving faster he might close the gap and get his hands on the bearded man. He figured he would be able to beat a guy as fat as that if it came down to a dash.

So he broke into a jog, keeping his body low. His eyes peered into the distance, hunting for anything up ahead. His ears strained to pick up the sound of footsteps other than his own.

Then he saw something. A speck of light down the track, getting brighter every second. And he heard a distant roar.

A train. Heading straight at him.

He almost tripped as he came to a stop.

Desperately he looked back at where he'd come from. He could barely see the glow from the platform. He had lost his sense of space and time in the heat of the chase. His stomach did a flip as he realized he had no chance of getting back in time.

The train light was growing larger and larger, like a giant eye. The engineer was sure to see him, he thought. The train was bound to slow down.

But even as he thought it, he could see how

wrong he was. If anything, the train was coming at him faster and faster, as if it were behind schedule, trying to catch up.

The light was blinding. The roar was deafening.

There was no way the train could stop now.

No way out for him.

No way but to die!

Chapter

5

JOE WASN'T THE only one staring with horror at the approaching train.

Frank was staring at it too. He felt as though his blood was draining from his body. Cold sweat beaded his skin. "Joe!"

He had returned to the platform right on schedule. But he wasn't surprised when he didn't find Joe waiting for him. Joe wasn't one to keep to schedules.

Frank sighed. He had just decided that he'd have to go down the tracks to find Joe. He was lowering himself onto the track when he heard the train. Jerking himself back up onto the platform, he watched helplessly as the train approached. He pretended he would see it slow down, see it come to a stop before the inevitable happened.

It didn't.

It didn't stop until it reached the platform and slowly screeched to a halt.

Frank stood in the middle of the stream of passengers pouring out of the train.

His eyes were dulled, his expression blank, his mind empty except for the single word that kept echoing inside it.

Joe. Joe. Joe.

Joe had lost his head one time too many. And now he had lost his life.

"Hey, what are you standing there for? No time to waste thinking. Get moving!"

Frank blinked. It was as if he could hear Joe's voice. He had to get a grip on himself.

"Didn't you hear me? Come on!"

Then Frank saw him. Joe was coming out from behind the last car in the train. He was motioning for Frank to join him—fast.

Frank was a long-distance runner, not a sprinter like his brother, but he set a personal-best record racing down the platform.

"I thought for sure you were a goner," he panted.

"Me too," said Joe.

"How did you—?"

"I'll show you," Joe said. "Come on."

After a quick check to make sure that the last few people had left the platform and no employees were watching, Joe and Frank squeezed behind the train and dropped back onto the tracks. Joe led the way into the darkness, using the faint glow from his flashlight. Frank used his flashlight too, and for five minutes they walked the tracks.

Frank felt confused. "I still don't see—"

"Take a look at this," Joe interrupted. He shone his light onto the side of the concrete tunnel wall. There, painted the same color, was a metal door.

"When I saw the train coming and realized it wasn't going to stop, I did the only thing I could," said Joe. "I hit the wall. Only instead of the wall I found this door. And even better than that, I found—well, look."

Joe pushed, and the door swung in.

"You don't have to tell me it was dumb luck. I know it was," said Joe, and Frank nodded.

"I'm not just talking about saving my life," Joe went on. "Finding this puts us back on the trail of that guy we were chasing. It must be the way he escaped. Come on. But watch your step. Right after we go through this doorway we go down some stairs."

"How far down do the stairs go?"

"I don't know," said Joe. "I figured I'd better go back to get you before trying to find out. Sometimes you actually come in handy in situations like this. If that guy has pals down there, I'd really need you. Besides, he probably stopped running once he ducked out of the tunnel. No way he could know I'd stumble on this door. Ordinarily, I wouldn't have spotted it in a million years. It looks like it's part of the wall."

"I'm not sure how safe this is," said Frank, feeling suspicious. "Why didn't the guy lock the door? Maybe we're walking into a trap."

"Sometimes you're too cautious for your own good," said Joe in disgust. He shone his flashlight on the inside of the door. Rust had completely corroded the bolt that would lock the door. But the bolt had been chiseled away so that it could be opened, and now there was no way to lock it again.

"Any more questions?" Joe asked.

Without waiting for Frank's reply, he headed down rusted metal stairs, which led into pitch darkness.

Frank did have more questions. He sensed that danger waited for them at the bottom of those stairs, and he would have liked to have some clue about what that danger would be. But he followed anyway.

The stairs went down and down.

"Wonder what they were used for," Joe said, calling back.

"There's a lot of stuff underground in the city. Basements built to house the foundations of all the tall buildings. Tunnels for drainage, water, electrical and communication cables. And under Grand Central Station there's a whole maze of maintenance sheds and storage rooms. Things keep changing so fast in the city that a lot of underground support systems have simply been abandoned. New York isn't into looking back. It's too busy rushing into the future."

"Hey, how do you know so much about it?" asked Joe.

"From that article I told you about."

Joe shook his head. "You're the only person I know who reads everything and forgets nothing. I hope you realize that computer data banks are making you obsolete."

"Speaking of data banks, I read—"

"Forget it," said Joe. "Time to get back to business."

They had reached the bottom of the stairs and found themselves in a corridor. The air was thick and musty. They guessed that no one had breathed it for years. But when their flashlight beams moved over the floor, they could see footprints in the dust.

Instinctively they put their fingers to their lips and grinned at each other, nodding. Then, in dead silence, they moved down the corridor.

There was a glimmer of light ahead. As they came closer, they saw that the light came from around the edges of a door that was slightly ajar.

Joe looked at Frank. Frank looked at Joe. Joe motioned for Frank to stay back to provide backup support. Then he slowly pushed the door open.

Putting his pen flashlight back in his pocket, Joe stepped into the room.

"What the—?" he said. "Frank, take a look at this."

Frank followed him in. "It's like a hospital ward," he said.

"Complete with a patient," said Joe.

The room they were in contained four hospital-type beds. In one of them lay an old man with his eyes closed, completely still.

"He's alive," said Frank, anxiously checking for a pulse. "But barely. The pulse is very slow, very weak."

Joe was staring grimly at the far wall—or, rather, at the coffin leaning there. "Are you thinking the same thing I am?" he asked.

Frank looked up from the sick man. "That videotape. Dad lying there, just like this. In that coffin."

"Hey, these aren't ordinary hospital beds," said Joe, examining one more closely. "Look at this."

Each of the beds, including the one that the comatose man was lying in, was equipped with straps to bind hands and feet.

Frank's face twisted. "It's like some kind of torture chamber." He looked at the other beds. Three of them were made up, their sheets and pillows unwrinkled. But the sheets on the remaining bed were in disarray, the pillow still revealing the imprint of a head.

Frank put his hand palm-down on it. "It's still warm," he said. "They must have grabbed whoever was lying here and carried him away. And I have a good hunch who that person was."

"Dad," said Joe, staring at the straps.

"Keep your cool," Frank cautioned him. "We can't help Dad by getting mad. What we have to get are clues about what's going on." He looked around the room. "There's one. Look."

He pointed to a small hole high in one of the walls. In the hole a lens glinted.

Frank made a closer inspection. "A camera lens. I have a hunch it's the same camera that took those pictures of Dad."

Joe pressed his ear to the wall. "I can hear it whirring. It must be shooting us right now." He picked up a scalpel that was lying on a bedside table and drove the scalpel into the hole. But the lens didn't shatter. Instead, the force of the blow pushed the camera backward, away from the opening.

"The camera must be in an adjoining room," said Frank. "Let's check it out."

In the corridor again, they cautiously approached the next room and entered.

Snapping on a light switch, they saw that the room was deserted. The video camera lay on the floor, pointing upward and still whirring.

Frank clicked it off and removed the film. "Kajimaki," he said. "This is the camera they used to tape Dad, all right. And now they're using it as a security system, to check out anyone who enters the room."

"How do we keep them from knowing we got in here?" Joe asked. "As long as the kidnappers think that the guy we chased gave us the slip, they won't feel pressured into giving up a bargaining chip like Dad."

"That camera store is just about to make another sale of Kajimaki film. We put the film in the camera, put the camera back on its mounting, and start it up again. When the kidnappers check it, all they'll see is a videotape of an empty room." Frank started for the door. "Let's go before they come back."

The boys left the room and hurried up the stairs. "The only trouble is," Joe remarked, "after we do all this, we won't be any closer to rescuing Dad."

"But with any luck, we will be soon," said Frank. "After we set up the camera again, we'll wait in the dark corridor for someone to check out the film. Then we'll tail him. If you can stand the wait," Frank kidded, "we might finally see some action."

"I hope so," said Joe, not responding to the teasing. "Because I get cold chills thinking what will happen to Dad if time runs out."

"Not to mention what will happen to all those other thousands of people in the city," said Frank.

*   *   *

It took fifteen minutes to get back to the camera store. After getting the videotape, Frank bought a manila envelope and some stamps.

"Give me all your ID," he told his brother. "If we have bad luck and get caught, we don't want the crooks to know our names and connect us with Dad. At least he won't pay for our fouling up."

Joe nodded and emptied his wallet. Frank put all the ID into the envelope, addressed the envelope to their home, put stamps on it, and dropped it into the mailbox. "Great," Joe said. "Now we're stripped for action."

A half-hour later he and Frank had set up the camera again and were crouched in the pitch-dark corridor. "If we could just *do* something," Joe whispered.

"All we can do is wait," said Frank. "And keep our eyes and ears open."

Then Joe heard something, the slightest of sounds, the faint rustling of someone's clothing, maybe the sole of a shoe brushing the floor. But to Joe's keyed-up senses, it sounded as if an alarm were going off.

He whirled around, his right fist ready, then lashed out as he faced a dim shape poised to jump him.

The shiver that went down his arm told him he had made solid contact with a jaw. And the figure toppling backward confirmed his observation.

At the same time, Frank had swiveled around

to find a blunt instrument being thrust down at him. He grabbed the wrist of the hand holding the weapon, flipped the man it belonged to, and, without breaking his flow of movement, delivered a knockout chop to the back of the man's neck.

"Close call," said Joe. He was breathing hard. "They almost got us."

"But now we have *them*. Come on," Frank said. "Let's get them onto those hospital beds and strap them down before they come to. After that we'll have time to figure out how to make them talk."

"It'll be a pleasure," said Joe. He was bending over to pick up the man he'd knocked out. Frank was doing the same with his man.

Unfortunately, this time when they heard sounds and saw dim shapes coming at them from the darkness, their hands were full.

All they had time to do was drop their burdens and begin to straighten up into fighting positions before time ran out on them.

Then blackness. Blackness filled with pain as hard rubber truncheons were hammered down on their skulls.

Chapter
6

THE BLACKNESS TURNED to glaring light. Joe's head hurt unbearably as he opened his eyes.

Groaning, he tried to touch the sore spot on his skull. But he couldn't move his hands—or his feet.

There was no need to look down. He could feel the straps cutting into his wrists and ankles. Turning his head, he saw that Frank was pinned the same way on the next bed.

Frank had already come to. When he saw Joe turn his head, he gave his brother a wry smile.

"Finally," a voice said. "We thought you two would never wake up."

The man who spoke was tall and pale faced. He wore his long black hair in a ponytail. Drooping on either side of his mouth was a long and straggly mustache. A not-so-white T-shirt and olive green army-surplus fatigue pants completed his sinister look. Beside him stood a powerfully built black man whose huge muscles rippled under a navy blue T-shirt. The man's massive legs were crammed into worn blue jeans.

Both men were looking at the Hardy boys with hatred.

They seemed to be restrained from violence only by the man who stood behind them. This third man was short and slight. His tan summer suit, pale blue button-down shirt, and striped tie contrasted sharply with his companions' clothes.

"Take it easy," he said to the other two. The authority in his voice was unmistakable. "Remember, we want to keep these two alive and conscious—for the time being, anyway. We need information from them."

Reluctantly the two stepped back, and their boss moved in toward Joe and Frank.

"What makes you think you can get away with this?" Joe demanded before the man had a chance to speak.

Frank interrupted, saying, "Look, I don't know what you think we did, but there's been a big mistake. My brother and I were sight-seeing," he began, desperately trying to concoct a story. "We got bored with all the usual tourist stuff. I remembered reading a newspaper article about all the underground space beneath Grand Central, and we figured it'd be fun to explore. We didn't know we'd be trespassing, honest. We're really sorry."

A nasty expression appeared on the suited man's face. "Stop wasting your breath lying, kid," he said. Then he shrugged. "But I guess it doesn't matter. Pretty soon you won't have any breath to waste. Down here we can get rid of you two without a trace in the time it takes to break your necks, which is exactly what Jack and Carl here are aching to do." He glanced at his two companions, and they looked more than pleased with the idea. Then he went on. His voice was gentler now, coaxing. "Come on, tell us how we can get our hands on the antibody to fix up Ian here, and we'll let you go. Otherwise, we'll make you wish you were as dead to the world as he looks now."

"Ian?" said Frank.

"Who's Ian?" echoed Joe.

But all they had to do was follow the man's eyes to see who Ian was—the man they had found lying as if dead. He was still there, in the bed on the other side of Frank.

"You must have thought you were real smart, leaving our friend here as bait," the man in the tan suit said. "You figured we'd come for him, while you were waiting outside ready to close in on us. What you didn't count on was that we'd be suspicious and hold back until we made sure everything was safe. Good thing we did. We spotted you taking your stakeout positions—and now you're the ones caught in your own trap."

Frank's mouth dropped open in surprise. "Hey," he said excitedly, "I think there's been some kind of mistake."

"Yeah, and you made it," said Carl, flexing his huge hands as if straining against an invisible leash.

"We're not the guys you think we are," Frank went on. "We're fighting the guys that did this to Ian—the same as you are."

"Right," Joe broke in. "I'm Joe Hardy, and this is my brother, Frank. We're from Bayport. If you don't believe it, just look in our—" He stopped abruptly.

"We did look in your wallets," the man in the suit said, finishing Joe's thought. "No ID. Two punks with orders not to be identified in case of trouble."

Frank tried another tack. "Look, if you think we're punks, why aren't we carrying weapons? If you searched us, you must know we're clean."

"I know what you did to our two friends back there in the corridor. Knocked them cold. You beat up helpless homeless people. But what you didn't figure was that we'd fight back."

Frank looked puzzled. "What do you mean," he said, " 'homeless people'?"

"Enough talk," Jack said. "Time for action."

The man in the suit nodded. "Jack's right. You two punks have jerked us around long enough. Tell us how we get our hands on the antibody, or I unleash Jack and Carl on you." His face was grim. "It's better to talk now than scream later."

"Believe me," Frank said, "we'd tell you about the antibody if we knew anything about it."

"You have to believe us," Joe pleaded. Then, as Jack and Carl moved forward, his desperation turned to pure anger. "You're jerks, you know that? Total jerks. We want that antibody as much as you do. They've snatched our dad and turned him into the same kind of zombie as Ian here. We could all help each other. But instead, you morons want to get rid of us."

The man in the suit held up a hand and stopped Jack and Carl from moving any closer to the Hardys.

"You know, I'm beginning to believe you," he said thoughtfully. "Not so much your words, but your anger. It sounds too real to be faked."

Frank gave his brother a grateful look. For once, Joe's hair-trigger temper had come in handy.

"Why don't you tell me more about yourselves, so I can check it out," the man said.

"Now you're talking sense," said Joe.

"Or else they're fast-talking us," said Frank. "Let's not be too eager to tell these guys anything. I mean, we know who *we* are. But how do we know who *they* are? Maybe they're pulling a scam on us. Maybe you've told them too much already."

Joe turned to the man in the suit. "All right. Who are you guys?"

"And can you prove it?" Frank added.

"So," said the man. "Now we're stuck." He grinned. "You don't trust *us*, and we don't trust *you*."

"It's like some kind of standoff," Frank agreed. "Neither one of us will let his guard down."

"The question is, how do we end it?" said the man.

But they didn't have time to come up with an answer.

"Okay, scum, up with your hands," a voice from the doorway ordered.

Standing there was the big, bald, bearded man whom Frank and Joe had chased. Behind him was a squat man with a military crew cut. Each held a .45—big and deadly looking.

There was no arguing with those guns.

Jack, Carl, and the man in the suit raised their hands instantly.

While the squat man held his gun on them, the bearded man walked over to Joe and Frank.

"Hey, kids, we meet again," he said with a nasty smile. "Congratulations. You finally caught up with me." He gave Frank, then Joe, a close-up view of his gun. "Notice that the safety is off," he said menacingly. "And let me tell you that this piece has a hair trigger. So don't make any quick movements when I unstrap you. Just keep lying there, deadlike, until I tell you to get up. I'd hate to have to get those nice clean sheets all stained with blood."

With his gun in one hand, he unstrapped first Joe, then Frank. Then he stepped back a safe distance and motioned for the boys to stand up.

Frank and Joe exchanged quick glances. This guy was a pro. It was going to be hard to get his gun away from him.

In fact, it might be impossible.

"Get over there!" the bearded man ordered, motioning Joe and Frank to join Jack, Carl, and the man in the suit.

The man in the suit spoke quietly to Joe and Frank. "Allow me to introduce myself," he said. "My name is Jones. Peter Jones. At least we can trust each other now. That's *one* problem we don't have."

Though Jones had spoken in a low voice, the bearded man caught the last sentence.

The gunman grinned. "You guys ain't going to have *any* problems to worry about," he said. "You see these guns? They're going to solve all your problems forever."

Chapter

7

"WE DO IT now, huh?" asked the man with the crew cut. His voice was eager.

"Cool it, dimwit," said the bearded gunman. "We got our orders. We take them to the dumpoff spot. That way, no stress, no mess."

The first gunman gave him a sour look. "Okay," he said. "Let's go."

"Out into the corridor," the bearded man told his captives. "And no funny business. Or else the dum-dum bullets in this gun will splatter you all over the walls."

The Hardys, along with Peter Jones, Jack, and Carl, were herded out of the room and down the corridor.

"That's far enough," announced the bearded man.

While his sidekick held a gun on the prisoners, he lifted a trapdoor in the floor, shone his flashlight through it, and disappeared down a metal ladder.

"Okay." His voice echoed from below. "Send them down. I'll cover them when they get here."

"You heard him," said the short-haired gunman, shining his flashlight in the hole.

"Where does this go?" Joe wondered aloud as he climbed down the ladder after Frank.

Peter Jones answered from above him. "You'll find out soon enough," he said. Obviously, Jones knew the answer, and he wasn't happy with it.

Frank looked around at the huge concrete tunnel they were standing in. "Looks like an abandoned sewer," he said, turning to Jones. "Am I right?"

"No talking!" the bearded gunman said before Jones could answer. "Keep your mouths shut and your ears open. That way, you won't die ahead of schedule."

By then everyone had reached the bottom of the ladder. Without hesitating, the gunmen marched their prisoners through the sewer. The silence was disturbed only by the sound of their footsteps.

"We're almost there," the bearded man reported. "If you have any prayers or goodbyes, say them now. You've got three minutes left."

The words seemed to reverberate in the air, and Joe felt a chill run through him. Then he realized it wasn't echoes he was hearing, but a distant roaring sound that was growing louder.

The two gunmen heard it too. Puzzled looks spread across their faces.

Jones and his companions did not look puzzled, though. Even in the dim glow of the flashlights, Joe could see their expressions light up with sudden hope.

A few seconds later the roaring was nearly deafening. Despite themselves, the gunmen turned around to see what was happening. At that same moment, Joe and Frank felt hands on their arms, pulling them up another ladder.

"Climb!" Jones shouted.

"Hold it or we'll—" the bearded gunman threatened, but his words were drowned out.

By that time Joe and Frank were well up the rungs of the ladder, following Jones and his friends.

The gunmen's flashlights had gone out, and the tremendous roaring filled the blackness below. But the five continued climbing.

From above, Frank and Joe heard a series of groans and then a harsh, grating sound just before a circle of dim light appeared. Water splattered down on the Hardys' upturned faces.

Jones and his friends had managed to remove a manhole cover and were climbing up through the opening.

Soon Joe and Frank stood beside them on a one-way city street blocked off from traffic by two huge garbage trucks positioned at the entrance. Rain pounded their bodies while gigantic forks of lightning lit up the black afternoon sky.

"I still don't get what happened down there," Joe said to Jones after they had replaced the cover and moved onto the sidewalk. "Maybe you can fill me in."

"You were right about our being in a sewer," said Jones. "But it wasn't an abandoned one. It was a storm sewer, built to carry off rain water from the streets. It's lucky for us that this storm hit when it did. Or else *we'd* be in the East River, and not those goons." Jones pointed down the street. "The river is just a couple of blocks from here. They were planning to knock us off and drop us in."

"I'm glad they're gone, but now we're left with no clues. We have no idea who those men were and who their boss is—unless you know," said Frank.

"I was hoping *you* did," Jones said.

Frank had to laugh. "Give us a break. Joe and I don't even know who *you* are."

"That's true," Jones agreed. "I guess we're all in the dark."

By then the sun was breaking through the clouds, flooding the city with dazzling light that reflected off the puddles in the street.

"Look," Jones said suddenly. "We'd better start putting our heads together—if we want to get anywhere, that is. My apartment's near here.

Let's go there, dry off, and exchange information. I've got a hunch we can help one another."

"Fair enough," said Frank.

"I'll fill you in at our next meeting," Jones said to both his men. They nodded.

Jack reached into his pocket and pulled out a small tool. He inserted it into a hole in the manhole cover and heaved. The cover lifted. Jack stood for a second, tilting his head with one ear toward the hole. "The water's only a trickle now. We can go back down in a minute." The man grinned broadly. "See you, Jonesy."

Joe and Frank exchanged glances. Go back down?

"Come on, kids, let's get going," Jones said before they could ask questions.

They left Jack and Carl standing by the manhole. "They're a little uncomfortable at my place," Jones explained. "It's too high up for them."

Jones's apartment was high up by anyone's standards, on the fortieth floor of a new high-rise.

"This is a long way up from that sewer down there," said Joe after they had dried off. He stood by a huge picture window and looked out over the city. The sun was just starting to dip below the tops of the high buildings to the west.

"Not so long—just two years long," said Jones. "But I'll tell you about myself later. First tell me about yourselves."

Frank and Joe did. They told him who they were, who their father was, and what had happened to them since the evening before.

"Your turn now," said Frank.

"Yeah," said Joe. "What did you mean about this apartment being two years away from that sewer down there?"

"I meant that two years ago I was living below the surface of the city."

"With Carl and Jack?" asked Frank.

"With them and with a lot of other people," said Jones. "Do you have any idea how many people live in forgotten building basements? In abandoned subway stations? In utility tunnels that are no longer used? There's practically an entire city underground."

"Why would anyone live like that?" Joe asked. "Like some kind of mole?"

"There are as many different reasons as there are people," said Jones. "But most of them just can't afford the rents in New York. They either lost apartments when their buildings were torn down to make way for luxury apartments or when their living spaces were turned into co-op apartments and condos for the well-to-do. Others simply got in one kind of jam or another and decided to drop out. Some of the people I know prefer to lead lives outside the mainstream. As I said, there are all kinds of people down there."

"And you?" said Frank.

"Me? I was a lawyer with a great career, a wife

and child I loved, and everything going for me. Then my wife and child died in an air crash, and nothing seemed worth doing. I wound up living underground with the others, sleeping on a cot in a room that once had been used for train maintenance. The only time I surfaced was to panhandle a few bucks and buy what I needed to live."

"But you've surfaced now," said Joe.

"After a while the wounds healed. I got a job, and since then I've done pretty well. But I never lost my ties with the people I lived with down below," said Jones. "And when the trouble started, they came to me for help."

"The trouble?" said Frank. "You mean those two goons who almost rubbed us all out?"

Jones nodded. "They're part of it. About five months ago, thugs started appearing underground. They drove people out with threats or actual violence. And since then, they've continued expanding their turf. Don't ask me why, but they want space and privacy, and their victims haven't been able to do anything to stop them. When the goons kidnapped Ian—the poor guy you saw lying in the hospital bed—to use in some kind of medical experiment, that was the last straw. There was a meeting to organize a self-defense corps, with me as coordinator."

"Couldn't they go to the cops?" asked Frank, and then answered his own question. "No, I guess they couldn't. Living underground is illegal, right?"

"Right," said Jones. "There's an unspoken agreement between the underground people and the cops. The people stay out of sight and out of trouble, and the cops stay out of their hair."

"So you guys don't want the cops getting mixed up in this fight any more than we do," said Frank.

"You've got the picture. The underground people are sure that if they called the cops in, the cops would have no choice but to destroy their life below."

"That leaves us with nobody to help us but each other," said Joe. "I just wish we knew who the enemy is."

"And what he's out to do," said Frank.

Just then the phone rang.

Jones answered it and listened a moment. Then he hung up, his face flushed with excitement. He turned to the Hardy boys.

"Come on. We finally got a break!" he said eagerly.

"What is it?" Joe asked.

"We managed to capture one of *them*. I want to question him." Jones hurried to the door. "I just hope we get there before they lynch him!"

Chapter

8

"WHY ARE WE wearing these?" Joe rapped his knuckles against the blue hard hat he was wearing. Jones had produced three of them as they rushed from his apartment. "Are we supposed to blast the truth out of this guy?"

"You'll see," Jones said.

They left the building, and he led the way down a quiet side street. Halfway down the block, he stopped at a manhole cover and opened his briefcase. Out came a crowbar. Jones wedged it in the cover, stamped down, and levered the cover out of the way.

"After I surfaced, I needed a convenient way to get back underground whenever I wanted," he explained. "I found out that if I wore a hard hat nobody would look twice when they saw me going down into a manhole."

After a few minutes of walking through a storm sewer, Jones said, "This is where we get out." He shone his flashlight up a short metal ladder, which they climbed.

They found themselves in a concrete cavern lit by candles. Three men in ragged clothes were guarding a man who clearly had gotten the worst of a fight.

"Good work," said Jones. "And thanks for getting in touch with me so fast."

"This guy made it easy—he supplied the phone," said one of the guards. "It's tapped into a telephone cable down here. A real neat job. I should know, I used to work for the phone company before they laid me off."

A thought struck Frank. "Just where in the city are we right now?"

"Under the center of Lexington Avenue, between Forty-second and Forty-third streets," said the man.

"That explains it," said Frank.

"Explains what?" Jones looked quizzical.

"The police chief's phone-tracing system pinpointed a threatening phone call coming from here," said Frank. "Peterson will be happy to know that his system wasn't at fault. But one thing I don't understand," he continued, "is how we can be under the middle of a major avenue. Maybe that's a dumb question, but—"

"Don't be hard on yourself," Jones interrupted. "You don't know how New York skyscrapers are built. First, builders have to dig huge basements to house the foundations. Those basements interlock with each other and extend under most of the city's streets."

"Well, you weren't kidding about there being a lot of empty space down here," said Joe, looking around him.

Jones's expression hardened. "There is a lot of territory down here," he said. "But not enough for *us* and *them*."

"Right," said a man wearing an old army jacket. "It's a war between the underground and the underworld—and we're going to win it."

"Remember, we just *think* our enemies are part of the underworld," cautioned Jones. "We don't have any proof they're professionals."

"We do now," said the man, indicating their prisoner. "This guy's a jailbird. His name's Gus Hays. We didn't get much more out of him. We figured we'd give you a crack at questioning him before we got really rough."

Jones nodded. He turned to Hays. "You heard the man. Why don't you tell me all you know—otherwise I can't answer for the consequences. It's not that *I'm* into violence, you understand. But these other gentlemen"—Jones gestured at the ragged bunch of men standing guard—"they get their kicks out of breaking bones."

Hays took a bloodstained handkerchief away

from his battered nose. "They can break every bone in my body," he said, "but I can't tell them any more than I have already."

"What did you tell them?" asked Jones.

"That I got out of the slammer a couple of months ago and was hired to do telephone taps and feed-ins like this one." Gingerly the man touched his nose.

"Who hired you?" asked Jones.

"I don't know." Hays shook his head slowly. "The day after I got out, some guy I didn't know called me. He arranged a meet and made me a job offer. He told me that if I did what I was told and didn't ask any questions I'd get my pay in cash in the mail every week. How could I say no?"

"If that's all you have to tell us, you're in big trouble," Jones snapped convincingly. "I don't think I can hold these men back much longer."

"But what else *can* I tell you?" Hays pleaded.

"For starters, what were you doing down here just now?"

"I was given another message to send to the police chief," said Hays.

"What was it?"

"I was supposed to remind him that time is running out for the city."

"That's all?" said Jones.

"That's all, I swear," Hays said. By now his face was pale and beaded with sweat. The men guarding him were closing in.

"Maybe I'm soft, but I believe you," said

Jones. "Now the question is, what do we do with you? We can't let you go."

"P-please—" Hays was completely losing it.

"There is an alternative: an all-expense-paid vacation underground—in *our* part of the underground," Jones said. "You don't leave till we tell you. Okay?"

"Sounds fine to me," Hays said. Accompanied by two burly guards, he walked quickly down the tunnel.

Jones watched them disappear. "Not much help," he said. "But at least we know the odds we're facing. Whoever we're fighting has criminal connections, lots of money, and a highly developed organization."

"That makes the threat against the city even more of a sure thing," said Frank. "And as the message said, time is running out. We have to move fast. Maybe we should split up. You and the underground people keep the fight going down here. Joe and I will hunt aboveground. We can keep in touch and coordinate our moves."

"Fair enough," said Jones. He gave Frank a card. "These are my numbers, at home and in the office. If I'm not there, use my answering machine."

"Good luck down here," said Frank.

"Good luck up there," said Jones.

Twenty minutes later, after one of the underground men had guided the Hardy boys through a maze of sewers and abandoned steam pipes back to Grand Central Station, Joe asked Frank, "Well, what's the next step?"

"The next step is to stop moving and start thinking," said Frank.

"I should have known you'd come up with something like that." Joe grimaced. "But let's not take too long doing it, okay?"

"We don't *have* too long," Frank reminded him. "But let's fuel up." He indicated a pizza stand in the station arcade. "We haven't had anything since breakfast, and it's way past dinnertime now."

Joe and Frank got on with their discussion between mouthfuls of pizza topped with green peppers, onions, pepperoni, and extra cheese.

"What we have to do is analyze this case," said Frank. He reached for the crushed red peppers. "What's the most mysterious thing about it?"

Joe shrugged. "As far as I'm concerned, everything."

"But what seems to make no sense at all?" Frank pursued.

Joe considered. "The whole way this blackmail scheme was set up. Why did the crooks put the muscle on the police chief and not on the mayor? And why did they snatch an out-of-towner like Dad?"

Frank nodded. "Just what I was thinking. There's hope for you yet."

"Please. Don't overwhelm me with compliments while I'm eating," warned Joe lightly. He finished his slice and signaled to the counterman to heat up another. "Anyway, tell me what else you were thinking."

"What Dad and Peterson have in common," said Frank, forgetting the half-eaten slice in his hand, "is that they used to work together years ago. Maybe this has something to do with that."

"But what?" asked Joe. "And how can we find out? We can't go to Peterson. There's no telling what kind of surveillance they have him under."

"Right. We can't alert them—or it's goodbye Dad." Frank put down his pizza, his appetite gone. "And goodbye city."

"So what do we do? Where do we go?"

"As the saying goes, there's no place like home." Frank was already pulling out a train schedule from his pocket. "We're in luck. A train leaves in four minutes. We can just make it."

"But my pizza!" Joe said, grabbing the slice and throwing down some money. Pizza in hand, he kept up with his brother and leaped aboard the train just as it was moving off.

Just then, he figured out why they were going home. "I should have thought of it earlier," he said after they sat down in a nearly empty car. He took a bite of his pizza. It was still warm. "Dad's files. He has records of all his old cases, including some from when he was a cop."

"It'll feel funny breaking into his private files, but I figure he'll understand," said Frank.

71

"But what'll we say to Mom and Aunt Gertrude?"

"Nothing," said Frank. "They both should be asleep by the time we arrive. We'll sneak into the house, go to Dad's den, get the info we need, and head back to the city."

"I have to hand it to you, you do have a knack for making plans." Joe licked his lips, wishing they made pizza slices bigger. "Of course, whether or not they work is a different story."

This plan, though, had every indication of working perfectly.

Their house was dark when they arrived.

They let themselves in and moved through the rooms without making a sound.

Frank silently swung open the door to the den.

But then the silence was shattered, and the plan with it.

"Freeze!" a snarling voice commanded. "Or you're as good as dead!"

Chapter

9

JOE AND FRANK stared at the two men who had invaded their house. One of them held a long-barreled gun in his hand, and he was pointing at an attachment at the end of the barrel. "Know what this is, kids?" he asked.

"A silencer," said Joe.

"Smart," said the man. "Real good. I like bright kids. And if you're *really* smart, you won't make me show you how well this silencer works."

"I'm really smart," said Joe. "And so's my brother."

"Two smart kids. Good for you. Now to prove you're smart, show us how to unlock your dad's files—and fast," he ordered. The man's tone indicated that he was serious. So did the gun in his hand, pointed directly at Frank's head. The partner drew a gun of his own and covered Joe.

The boys' eyes met.

"I'm not going to argue," said Frank. He went to the desk and took out a key to the steel cabinets that contained Fenton Hardy's files. He turned the key in the pickproof lock and opened one of the drawers.

"Thanks for being so cooperative," said the first man.

"Yeah, you're real good kids," said the second.

"It's a shame we gotta do what we gotta do," said the first.

"But orders are orders," said the second. "And we were told what we had to do if anyone spotted us during this break-in."

"So long, kids," said the first as both men brought their guns into firing positions.

"Hey, wait a minute," Frank said, acting terrified. "You're not going to—?"

"Please! We're so young! Give us a break," said Joe. His voice was trembling.

"We'll do anything you ask, anything," said Frank.

"This can't be happening," said Joe. "It's a nightmare!"

"Come on," said the first intruder. "I thought you kids would have a little more guts than this."

"Yeah." The second man shook his head. "Kids today just don't have what it takes."

"You kids get hold of yourselves," said the first man. "Stop shaking, stand up straight, die like men."

"Please," begged Frank.

"Don't," begged Joe.

"Drop it, you two!" commanded a voice from the doorway.

Laura Hardy, the boy's mother, was standing there with a gun in her hand.

"Whoa!" said the first intruder, hastily dropping his gun. "Watch that thing, lady, it might go off!"

"See, I'm dropping my gun too," said the second man. He let it fall from his hand.

"I was starting to think you wouldn't get here," Frank said to his mom. "Good thing Dad had that alarm installed to go off in your bedroom if anyone got into his files without first shutting the system off."

"Joe, gather up those guns on the floor and cover these two. Frank, get some clothesline from the storeroom."

Soon the intruders were securely tied with gags in their mouths. "All right, Joe," said Mrs. Hardy, "we can put our guns down now and call the police to pick up this pair. Then, of course, you boys will explain to me what this is all about." She reached for the phone. "Gertrude told me you called and said you were staying in the city with your father."

"Hold it, Mom. Better not call the cops," Frank said quickly.

"Why not?"

"I didn't want to worry Aunt Gertrude, so there was something I didn't tell her."

Laura Hardy's eyes bored straight into her son's. "And what exactly did you leave out, young man?"

"That Dad was asked by his old pal Peterson to help out on a case," said Frank. "He said we could tag along, just to find out what detective work was all about."

"Is that so?"

"Yeah. Then it turned out that Dad needed information from his files, so he sent us here to get it. But it seems as if the guy he's hunting had the same idea."

"But I still don't understand why I shouldn't call the police." Laura Hardy was beginning to look confused.

Frank paused. Then he said, "You tell her, Joe."

Joe, his mind a blank, stared openmouthed at his brother. Fortunately, an idea came to him.

"Dad doesn't want the crook to know how close he is to being caught," Joe said, inventing quickly. "If these two are locked up, they'll call their lawyer, and their lawyer will alert their boss."

"That's right," said Frank, flashing Joe a grin of gratitude. "So what you have to do is hold on to these two bozos for a day or so, before we send them off to jail."

"Oh, come on, Frank—"

"We wouldn't ask you to do it, Mom, but we know you've helped Dad on cases before. And he's told us you're as tough in the crunch as he is."

Looking pleased, Laura Hardy nodded. "All right. I'll be glad to help out." She looked at the boys closely then. "Your father is all right, isn't he?" she asked.

Joe felt himself clench inside for what he was about to say. "Sure, Mom," he said. "Dad's doing great."

"Well, then"—Laura Hardy glared at the intruders—"I think it's best to put you two in the basement," she told them. "And I warn you— don't try anything. I might not like guns, but I do know how to use them."

The intruders were meek as lambs as Joe and Frank untied their feet and led them downstairs, with their mother holding a gun on them.

"If you two want to tell us who your boss is, we could tell the D.A. you were cooperative, and maybe your sentences could be made lighter." Laura Hardy's voice was brisk and professional.

The first intruder, sweat beading his brow, indicated that he wanted his gag removed. "Look, lady, if I knew anything, I'd tell you. But our boss keeps his identity secret. And we've only been working for him a couple of months."

"How did he get in touch with you, then?" Laura Hardy persisted. "No lying, or you'll be sorry."

"Mac and I were fresh out of jail when a man called us and asked us to work for him," said the second crook after Joe removed his gag. "We receive orders by phone and get paid by mail. Honest. It's the truth."

Laura Hardy raised her eyebrows. "I suppose I have to believe you. But if I find out you've been lying—"

"Not us," said the first man.

"No, ma'am," said the second.

"Oh dear," said a voice. "What's going on down there?" It was the boys' aunt Gertrude.

"Don't worry, Gertrude," said Laura Hardy, helping the boys gag and bind the men. "It's just the boys."

"I knew I heard noises down there," said Gertrude.

"They found a couple of strays," Laura Hardy said, repressing a smile. "We'll be keeping them in the basement until they go to the—pound."

"I hate strays," said Gertrude. "Don't expect me to go down there to feed them."

"I expected that reaction," Laura Hardy said as she and the boys went up the stairs. "It'll make things easier."

Joe rushed to the files and started working through them. "Dad said we should look in the stuff covering the time he was a New York City cop." He kept looking. "Hey, Frank," he said, "the files are arranged by year. Now all we have to do is search for the years when he was on the force."

"Your father started on the force twenty-five years ago," said Mrs. Hardy. "He decided to go off on his own when you two were still toddlers—about fifteen years ago, I think."

"Thanks, Mom," Frank said. He pulled the files covering that time period out of the file cabinet. They formed a thick stack of papers and newspaper clippings. Fenton Hardy had been a very busy cop.

"We'll need a couple of shopping bags for these," said Joe.

"You're taking them *all?*" His mother looked surprised.

"That's what Dad told us to do," said Frank. "Our job wasn't to ask questions."

"Then I won't bother asking any either," said his mom. "I'll wait until he gets home."

"We've got to get to bed, Mom, so we can go back to the city on the earliest train tomorrow morning."

"Okay. Well, sleep tight, boys. I think I'm ready to go back to bed too," she added with a yawn.

What neither boy mentioned was that they would be up all night going over the files, paper by paper, clipping by clipping.

Dawn was turning the New York City sky from purple to pink when the phone rang in Peter Jones's high-rise apartment.

Groaning, he reached for the receiver, sleep still fogging his mind.

But his thoughts became clear when he heard what Frank Hardy had to say.

"Sorry to wake you, Peter, but I thought you'd want to know—we've found out who our enemy is."

Jones was suddenly awake and on his feet. "Hey!" he said. "That's great!"

"Maybe," said Frank, his voice grim. "You'll have to decide that for yourself when you find out who we're up against."

Chapter

10

"THAT MAN'S A monster," Jones exclaimed as he looked at the photo on the yellowing newspaper clipping later that morning.

"Just what I said when I got a look at him," agreed Joe.

The man in the photo was tall and horrendously fat. Rolls of flab bulged over the starched collar of his shirt. Piglike eyes stared out at the camera. The handcuffs binding his wrists together clearly were cutting into his ample flesh.

"Mob Chief Collared by Rookie Cops," the headline above the photo read.

"Listen to the story," said Frank. He picked up another clipping. "This is from the inside of the same paper. It gives the details. 'Nick Trask was today taken into police custody by two first-year patrolmen, Fenton Hardy and Samuel Peterson, as the result of evidence gathered in an investigation carried out on their own initiative over the past several months. The charges against the reputed mob boss include loan-sharking, extortion, kidnapping, drug dealing, and assault. Trask has refused all comment, but his lawyer, William Sawyer, has issued a statement expressing confidence that the charges against his client will be proven baseless.' ''

"That lawyer was wrong, though," said Joe, showing Jones more clippings from the same file. "Trask was convicted on enough counts to send him up for twenty-three years—and for their work, Peterson and Dad made it to detective grade in a couple of years."

"Listen to this," said Frank, who read from another clipping. " 'After sentencing, Trask attempted to break free from his guards to attack the two policemen who had arrested him. Trask shouted a vow of revenge at the pair of patrolmen, saying he would get them no matter how long it took.' ''

Jones looked at the dates of the clippings. "Twenty-four years ago. Trask must have been released last year—unless he got time off for good behavior."

"He wasn't that lucky," said Frank. "The judge sentencing him said that no time off would be granted."

Jones nodded. "It all seems to fit. Trask got out a year ago."

"And now he's looking for revenge," said Frank. "And somehow in that year he's managed to recruit an army of crooks. I wonder where he got them all."

"I can make a good guess," said Frank. "Each of the three we've pumped recently got out of prison. He must have gotten to know a lot of men in his years behind bars. All he had to do was set up a kind of employment agency for them when they got out. He'd have a huge pool of skilled labor."

"But where did he get the dough to hire them?" wondered Joe.

"A big-time hood like Trask probably had quite a stash hidden away," said Jones. "That might explain what he and his gang are doing underground. He could have held on to his money, but no way could he have hung on to his territory. His fellow mobsters must have taken over his turf, and there would be no way they'd give it back."

"So he's using his supply of money and cheap labor to build a *new* crime empire," said Frank. "An underground empire this time—so big that it's scary." He shook his head. "And crazy, too. He'll wipe out the city, just for starters."

"If we could just find out where he's operating from, where his headquarters are," said Joe. "I could really go for busting in on him and getting my dad back."

"I have it!" said Frank.

"Have what?" said Joe irritably. Frank could never resist coming out with a teaser before explaining one of his bright ideas.

"I have thought of the place we can begin looking," said Frank. "The city has to have records, right? They probably even have a tie-in to federal prison records. In addition to Trask, I bet they'll have records of the others who were in with him and have since been released."

"They do have," said Jones, nodding. "It's all in a central computer bank downtown."

"If we could just get at it," said Frank.

"There's a chance we can," said Jones eagerly. "I'm going to make a phone call." When he returned later, he said, "We're in luck. The underground knows where Lardner is. They're sending him right up."

"Who's Lardner?"

"He's a computer expert, one who set up a lot of the city systems. But he was let go, right in the middle of a high-tech slowdown, and he wound up where he is now—in the underground." Jones glanced at his watch. "He should be here in a few minutes. *That* was the good news," he said.

Joe and Frank had been sitting down, and by the look on Jones's face, they were glad they had some support under them.

"The bad news," he went on, "is that Ian—you know, the old guy you found in the bed—he died."

Joe let his head fall back onto the top of his chair. "He died?"

"Yeah. Doc said that the bug the crooks used on him must have been a doozy."

"Dad—" Frank mumbled woodenly. "What kind of condition could *he* be in then?"

"Look," Jones said, "Ian was an old man—weak to begin with. Your dad's younger. He'll make it. You'll see."

The boys weren't sure. But they knew that feeling sorry for themselves would get them exactly nowhere.

"Doc?" echoed Frank, coming out of his fog. "Doc who? Who's he?" Then he said, "No, don't tell me. Doc dropped out of his medical practice for some reason or other, then disappeared into the underground."

His eyes twinkling, Jones nodded. "You're beginning to get an idea of how many different kinds of people live down there. There are a lot of ways to fail in the city. But there aren't many places to go if you do."

A little while later the door buzzer sounded.

"I hope this is the help we need," said Frank as Jones told the doorman to let the caller in.

A couple of minutes later a small man dressed in faded blue jeans walked into the apartment.

After the situation was explained to him, Lardner said, "Yeah, I designed the data bank myself. It has real easy access."

"But how do we get to it?" asked Frank.

"That's easy too," said Lardner. He pulled out a set of keys from his pocket. "When I got canned, I took these as souvenirs. These are the sweethearts that'll let us into the building and then into the computer room."

"What are we waiting for?" said Joe. "Let's go."

"First we have to make a plan," said Frank.

"Plan? What plan do we need?" asked Joe, his voice riddled with impatience. "Today's Sunday, in case you haven't noticed. Nobody'll be working down there. We'll sneak in, get the information, and get out. A piece of cake."

"Well, it's true we don't have much time," Frank said reluctantly.

"Then what are we waiting for?" said Joe eagerly.

Jones cleared his throat. "I hope you kids don't mind, but I'm not going with you."

Joe stopped in his tracks, surprised.

Jones looked embarrassed. "The risk is too great. If I were caught, I would be disbarred."

"That's okay, Peter, we can handle this ourselves," said Joe. "Frank is into computers."

"With Lardner's help, I don't see any problems," agreed Frank.

It was Lardner's turn to look embarrassed. "If it's all the same to you, I'd just as soon stay out of this too. I've been thinking about finding a job lately, and a jail record would finish me. So, how about if I just give you the keys and tell you everything you need to know."

"I understand," said Frank, nodding.

"Sure—no problem," said Joe. He meant it.

As he said to Frank on the taxi ride downtown, "It must be a drag being grown-up and having so much to lose that you're afraid to take risks."

"Yeah," said Frank. "Jones and Lardner aren't lucky like us. All we have to lose is our lives."

"Always worrying," said Joe.

Frank shook his head. "That's because there's always something to worry about. Sometimes I think it would be better to lead a slightly more normal life."

"Oh, come on, you know as well as I do you'd be bored to death if you didn't have a mystery to solve."

The expression on Frank's face remained serious. "This is one mystery I could do without. Risking my life is one thing. But it's Dad's life that's on the line now."

"Right," said Joe. The reality of what could happen to their father returned.

Just then the cab stopped in front of a large

building in lower Manhattan. "Let's go," Joe said, psyching himself. "This is going to be a snap. I can feel it."

"So far, so good," Frank admitted a quarter-hour later. "In fact, the whole thing—getting in the side door and up to this room—has been *too* easy."

"You're like one of those guys in the movies," said Joe. "You know, the ones who say, 'It's quiet here. *Too* quiet.' Come on, relax."

"I'll relax after I check out the access codes Lardner gave me," Frank said. "Too much might have been changed since he was let go." He sat down in front of a computer screen and looked at the piece of paper Lardner had given him. On it the computer whiz had printed very specific instructions. "Here goes," Frank said, and started punching out the first code.

"It's working!" he said ecstatically, and punched out Nicholas Trask's name.

Trask's case history flashed on the screen, including the name of the prison where he had served his time.

"Now for the next code," said Frank.

When he punched it out, he had access to the records at Trask's prison. He wrote down the names and addresses of prisoners who had been there during Trask's stay and who had been recently released.

"Interesting," he said. "Current addresses are supposed to be listed, but look at all the prisoners that have 'Address Unknown.' "

"I'll bet Trask recruited a lot of them," said Joe. "We'll have to track them down somehow."

"There's a listing of their families' addresses, and their wives'," said Frank, who was writing furiously. "That should help. Hey, look at that name. Helmut von Reich."

"What about him?" said Joe.

"I remember reading about von Reich," said Frank. "He was a doctor convicted of manufacturing some kind of phony cancer cure."

"I have to admit, sometimes your memory comes in handy," said Joe. "Although I hate to think what your brain must look like."

Frank was scanning the data on the doctor. "Von Reich was released almost at the same time as Trask. I think we can make an educated guess now about where Trask got his Virus A and Virus B."

"Yeah, I think you're right," Joe said. "And speaking of those viruses . . ."

"Time to go," said Frank, stuffing the sheets of paper covered with names and addresses into a pocket.

But the brothers made it only as far as the computer room door.

Joe reached for the knob. But the door swung open before he touched it.

89

"You kids find what you were looking for—or do you need some help?"

Two policemen blocked the doorway. Both had guns drawn.

Frank and Joe exchanged glances—they knew what they had to do.

"Look, before you start asking questions, take us to Samuel Peterson," said Frank. "We have information he desperately needs."

"Peterson? *The* Peterson, the chief of police?" one of the cops asked.

"Right," said Joe. "Hey! What are you waiting for? Why are you standing there grinning? I told you, this is urgent."

"Just hold your horses," said the second cop. "First, let's check what you've done to these computers."

"At least hurry up about it. We have to get to Peterson." That was all Frank could say.

The cop nodded but sat down at a computer. "It'll just take a minute," he said. While his partner kept a gun on the two brothers, he consulted a slip of paper and began punching keys furiously.

Frank watched data flash on the screen, then vanish. It was like seeing a neon sign that kept going on and off.

Then he realized what was happening.

"Hey, watch it!" he shouted. "You're erasing all that stuff!"

The cop at the keyboard didn't bother looking up. His partner with the gun answered for him.

"Yeah, kids, just like we're going to erase *you*."

Chapter

11

"DON'T WORRY," SAID the one with the gun. "We ain't going to rub you out—yet."

"First we have to take you to the boss," said the other one, snapping off the computer and standing up. "We don't do anything unless he gives the okay."

"But I have a hunch what he'll want us to do," said the first man. He laughed. "You kids better not make any plans for the future."

"Let's cut out of here now—before somebody finds that guard we stiffed," said his partner.

Joe and Frank were herded from the building. Nobody would think twice, seeing a couple of cops with their guns drawn covering two teens. But there was no one to notice. The early-Sun-

day-morning streets around the cluster of munici-
pal buildings in downtown Manhattan were deserted.

"Up here," said one of the men. They climbed
some broad steps leading up to a huge granite
building. In front of the building stood a large
statue of a woman who symbolized justice.

Joe and Frank exchanged glances. Why were
they being taken to a city courthouse?

The men let themselves into the building with a
key, then took the boys down to the basement in
an elevator. There they unlocked another door
and went down a flight of hidden steps to a long
underground corridor.

"Pretty slick, huh?" said one of the men, following the beam from his flashlight. "Last place
anybody would look—right under the biggest
courthouse in the city. Seems they built this
tunnel along with the building a hundred years
ago, and then they forgot about it."

"Even better is where it goes," said his partner.

"Don't even try to guess where, kids," said the
first thug. "You couldn't in a million years."

"Let me in on the big secret," said Joe sarcastically. "The suspense is killing me."

"Ain't going to be the suspense that kills you,"
said the first guy, chortling at his own joke.

"You can ask the boss himself," said his partner. "We're here."

They had reached a metal door at the end of the

tunnel, and one of the men gave a series of long and short rings on a buzzer, clearly a code.

The door swung open.

Joe and Frank barely noticed the man who opened it because they were staring past him at a man rising from behind a desk.

The guy looked like a body builder who had been stretched to six and a half feet. He was wearing a black T-shirt and black jeans that showed the enormous muscles of his arms, shoulders, chest, and thighs. Even his head looked like an enormous muscle, with its shaven skull gleaming in the light from the naked overhead bulb. Salt-and-pepper hair bristled over the top of his shirtline.

Who was this awesome character?

The same answer crossed both Frank and Joe's minds. But neither of them could believe it.

No way this rock-hard man could be the mountain of fat they had seen in the yellowing newspaper photo. No way they could be standing here staring at Nick Trask.

"Don't tell me who you kids are," the man said with a thick New York accent. "Let me guess. The Hardy boys. Congratulations. You moved faster than I figured you would."

"Hardy boys?" said Joe, putting on a tough New York accent himself. "Who you talking about?"

"You got us mixed up with somebody else, mister," said Frank with the same accent.

"Come on, kids, don't waste my time," said the well-preserved hoodlum. "If you're not the Hardy boys, I'm not Nick Trask."

"You, Nick Trask?" said Joe.

"Don't kid us," said Frank. "I mean, I heard stories about him. You know, like he's a legend in the neighborhood. A real big shot. And from what I heard, a real tub of lard too."

"That was a long time ago," said Trask. "Over twenty years you can build a lot of muscle if you pump iron day after day, getting in shape for when you get out.

"I was the youngest boss in the organization," he said. "I lived high, ate and drank everything I pleased. A great life. But two guys took it all away from me. Peterson—and *Hardy.*"

"Hey, Mr. Trask, you got the wrong guys. We ain't no Hardys," said Frank. "We was just fooling around in that office, you know, for kicks, when your guys jumped us."

"That's right, Mr. Trask, sir," said Joe. "You let us go, and we won't say a word. I mean, we think you're something. In our neighborhood you're a regular hero."

Trask turned to one of the phony cops. "Frisk these punk kids. Fast."

The man did as he was told. He came up with an old clipping about Trask that Joe had accidentally left in his pocket.

"Nice try, kids," said Trask. "I didn't even need this to know who you are. I already figured you went back home to get at your dad's files when the people I sent to snatch them didn't report back.

"When I figured you had your hands on the old clippings, I knew you'd use the city computers to check me out," Trask went on. "Well, both you kids were too smart for your own good. You didn't stop me from wiping out my records. And you gave me a bonus by giving me *you*."

"What good is having us going to do you?" said Frank.

"I ain't sure yet. But I'll figure out some—" Trask paused, and a smile made his face even uglier. "I just got an idea." He turned to the phony cops. "Go get the doctor. He's in the lab. I got a job for him.

"We installed a lab in the subbasement of the building next door. Pretty neat setup, huh?" said Trask.

A minute later his two men returned. In their custody was a slim, dark-haired man with a small goatee and big, bulging eyes. The man wore a spotless white lab coat, but his hands were stained multicolored by chemicals.

Joe took one look at him and thought he was a mad scientist, right out of central casting.

The guy's voice was mad, too, a different kind. Angry mad.

"I was just coming in to see you, Trask," he said. "I told you two days ago, I need more supplies. And the company will not give me what

I need if I do not pay. Do not promise me that you will have your men hijack the stuff. They have already made too many mistakes in what they have stolen."

"Look—" Trask started.

"I do not want excuses," interrupted the doctor. "I want to continue my experiments. You promised to give me all I need if I gave you what you want. I fulfilled my part of the bargain, and now you must keep your part. Or else no more virus."

"Your lab stuff is costing me a fortune, von Reich," Trask growled.

"You did not seem to worry about cash when we worked out our plan in the cell," the doctor said.

"How was I to know about inflation?" Trask muttered.

"Your financial problems do not interest me," the doctor said coldly. "I don't care how you get it, but I want my money. If you want to call our deal off, I can continue my experiments elsewhere."

Joe and Frank expected Trask to twist the doctor's head off. The look in his eyes said that he wanted to. Surprisingly, however, Trask forced a smile onto his face. He laid a huge hand on the doctor's narrow shoulder in a calming gesture.

"Hey, Doc," he said, "don't get mad. You'll get your money, and so will everybody else, as soon as the city comes through with the twenty million. And that will be just chicken feed compared to how much we'll rake in once we take over the whole underground. We'll be able to loot any store we want, transport any drug, set up illegal gambling, the works. We'll be as rich as kings. All we need is that twenty million to really put us into business. Just be patient a little while longer."

"I'll be patient—but still I need more money for my suppliers," said the doctor. "And they deal in cash only."

"Okay, okay," snapped Trask. "How's this?" He reached into his pocket and pulled out a roll of bills. Slowly he peeled them off and dropped them into von Reich's waiting hand. First hundred-dollar bills, then fifties, then twenties. Trask stopped with over half the roll still in his hand.

"That's all?" demanded the doctor.

"I got other expenses," Trask said quickly. He stuffed the roll back into his pocket, but not before Frank and Joe caught a glimpse of the top bill.

It was a single. The boys exchanged glances. They both realized that the bankroll had big bills on top, but the bulk of them were small. It looked as though Trask had a cash-flow problem.

The doctor, though, seemed satisfied. "Okay, for now we are back in business. I will go back to my work."

"First I got some more of *my* work for you. A couple of new patients, sons of Mr. Hardy," Trask said. "They need treatment real bad."

"Treatment A or Treatment B?" asked the doctor, a hint of a nasty smile edging across his thin lips.

"Treatment A," said Trask. "We'll save B for the big moment."

With guns leveled at them, the Hardy boys followed Dr. von Reich out of Trask's headquarters. They were escorted down a short corridor and into a room filled with laboratory equipment.

"You first," the doctor said to Frank. "Lie down on the table."

Frank glanced at the gun trained on him. He shrugged and then obeyed.

Furtively Joe looked sideways at the gun trained on him. He couldn't make a move.

One of the phony cops strapped Frank down on the table, then stepped back.

Meanwhile the doctor had filled a hypodermic with a solution drawn from a tube stored in a refrigerator.

Both Hardy boys knew what the solution was.

Despite himself, Frank grew pale. The doctor, smiling with evident enjoyment, held the instrument in front of Frank's eyes for a moment so that Frank could get a good, long look at it.

"What's the matter, little boy, afraid of a tiny needle?" the doctor asked mockingly. "Do not worry. You will hardly feel it. And then, I promise you, you will feel nothing at all."

Before Joe's horrified eyes, von Reich plunged the needle into Frank's arm. Almost instantly Frank's eyes bulged with shock and then closed just as fast, his face and body going slack.

"Just lay him on the floor. It will not bother him in the least," the doctor told one of Trask's men.

Two minutes later Joe was the one strapped on the table.

He steeled himself so he wouldn't flinch when the doctor gave him a close-up of the needle.

But he couldn't help shuddering inwardly when he heard the doctor's words: "As the saying goes, young man, like father, like sons."

Chapter

12

BLACKNESS.

That was all Joe saw. But he was sure he was awake. He was sure he had his eyes open.

Maybe this was what Virus A did to you, he thought. Maybe it took away your sight and made you think you were conscious when you were really still knocked out.

Was he running a fever? He didn't think so. But to make sure, he put his hand on his forehead. Or at least he tried to. He couldn't move.

He seemed to be tied up hand and foot, lying on what felt like the concrete floor of a pitch-dark room. But he had no idea what kind of room he was in.

Then the total silence was broken as he heard footsteps moving toward him. He tensed. He felt a foot collide with his side. Next a hand felt his face, forehead, nose, gagged mouth.

"That you, Joe?" It was Frank's voice that was whispering.

Joe felt the gag being taken out of his mouth.

Before Joe could say anything, Frank said hoarsely, "Keep your voice way down. This place might be bugged."

"Always playing it cautious," Joe teased softly. "See if you can untie me."

Frank untied Joe's wrists, then the rope around his ankles.

"Easy as pie," whispered Frank. "Whoever tied us up was never a Boy Scout. I think this underground living is getting to Trask's boys. They're getting sloppy."

"You were tied up too?" Joe asked. He tried to rub the circulation back into his wrists and ankles. "How did you get loose?"

"When I came to, I rolled along the floor, hoping I'd run into some luck," said Frank. "And I did. I hit a wall. Then I made my way along the wall until I reached a doorway. The door was locked, but it was set far enough into the wall to leave a hard edge exposed. I used the edge to saw through the ropes around my wrists. The rest was easy."

"Do you think Dad is tied up in here?" wondered Joe.

"I doubt it. I covered a lot of territory in here before I found you."

"How long do you figure we were knocked out?" asked Joe.

"No idea," said Frank. "That Virus A is strange. It put me out like a light, but now I don't feel bad at all. How about you?"

"All I feel is starved," said Joe.

"We're really in the dark about everything," mused Frank.

As if in answer to this, light from an overhead bulb flooded the room.

In that first flash of light, Joe and Frank stared at each other. Their faces were streaked with grime, their hair was dusty, their clothes looked like dirty rags, but no one else was in the dusty concrete room.

They didn't have time to talk. Without saying a word, they gave each other a nod, then dashed toward the door. There they pressed themselves against the wall on either side of the doorway.

Just then the door swung inward.

The two fake cops entered.

"Hey, where did those—?" was all the first one had a chance to say before Frank leaped on him from the rear. Joe took on the second man.

Three minutes later the Hardy boys had the unconscious men tied up and gagged.

"Quick!" said Frank. "Let's get out of here!"

They left the room, closing the door behind them, and found themselves in a dimly lit corridor that seemed familiar.

"I think the lab we were given the shots in is

down there," Frank said. They headed toward where Frank was pointing.

"This looks like it," said Frank as he and Joe stood facing the closed door.

Joe took a deep breath. "Here goes nothing," he said as he pushed the door open.

We've hit the jackpot, was Frank's first thought when he looked inside.

Inside the room, Dr. von Reich was without bodyguards, though he was not alone. Sitting in a chair, looking pale but wide awake, was Fenton Hardy.

The doctor was standing with his back to the boys in front of Mr. Hardy, a hypodermic in his hand. He was poised, ready to give the injection. Mr. Hardy was not tied up, but he was making no move to stop the doctor. Frank ran across the short distance and grabbed von Reich's wrist, forcing him to drop the needle to the floor. Joe, meanwhile, wrapped one arm around the doctor's neck and pressed his other hand across the doctor's mouth.

"Make a sound, and listen to your neck snap," Joe threatened. Frank closed the lab door and quickly returned to the doctor and frisked him.

"He's clean," Frank said, hurrying to his father's side.

"No funny business, or we'll lay you out," Joe warned. Then he released the doctor.

"Dad, are you okay?" Frank asked.

He had reason to be concerned. Fenton Hardy

had remained sitting in the chair. There was an expression in his eyes that his sons had never seen before. A bewildered, confused look.

"Okay? Yes, I'm okay," he said, but his voice was not reassuring. It was low, indistinct, as if he were having trouble getting his words out.

"It must have hit him harder than it did us," said Frank.

"You were figuring on shooting Dad up with more Virus A, huh?" he snarled. "And hitting us with it, too, I bet. That's why you sent the goons to get us. Well, unless you give us the antibody that cleans the bug clear out of Dad, I'm giving you a shot of your own medicine—or should I say, your own sickness."

Fear was apparent on von Reich's face, but the doctor couldn't resist giving the Hardy boys a superior sneer. "I thought you two were supposed to be bright. Hasn't one of you figured it out by now?"

"Figured what out?" asked Joe, looking at Frank for some clue about what the doctor was hinting at.

His brother didn't fail him. "I think I know," Frank said.

"And what do you know?" asked the doctor.

"Virus A doesn't exist," said Frank. "That would explain why we made such complete recoveries. And why Dad will, too, once he shakes off the effects of the drug you used on him."

"So you do have some semblance of intelligence, after all," the doctor said in an oily voice. "How reassuring to learn that not all of our young people are a bunch of—"

"Hey, wait!" Joe broke in unexpectedly. "What about Ian, the old guy we found underneath Grand Central? *He* didn't make a complete recovery."

"That's right," Frank agreed, turning from Joe to glare at the doctor. "The man's dead."

Dr. von Reich seemed genuinely puzzled. "I'm telling you the truth. There is no Virus A. I used a drug, not a virus. I don't know why he died."

The Hardys looked at each other. "So," Joe said, perking up, "if you have no virus, you've got nothing to threaten the city with."

"I'm afraid I have to disappoint you," said the doctor, wearing an evil-looking smile. "There may be no Virus A, but Virus B is very, very real. We merely decided that developing a Virus A was an unnecessary expense."

"So where is this Virus B kept?" Joe asked.

"Now, that, young man, I will not tell you. I must save something to bargain with. I will tell you, though, that you will never find it."

"I believe him. Let's go before somebody down here finds out what's up," said Frank.

"Yeah," said Joe. "I guess we can get the virus later. Get ready to move, von Reich.

"No, wait," he said, picking up the hypodermic from the floor and looking at it. "Good. It wasn't damaged. Let's see how fast this knock-out drug of yours works, Doctor."

"That's pretty gross," said Frank dubiously.

"What do you mean?" asked Joe. "It'll put von Reich out of action, won't it? We can really make time getting out of here and be back with help before Trask realizes we've gone and has time to do anything about Virus B. Besides, the drug won't do anything more than knock the doctor out for a while."

"Okay, Joe, I'll go along with your scheme. The question is, who gives von Reich the shot? I'm not into handling needles."

Joe looked at the hypodermic in his hand, and his stomach gave a lurch. "Me either." Then he smiled. "Good thing we have an expert in the room." Smiling, and despite the doctor's protests, he handed von Reich the hypodermic. "Doctor," Joe said, "show us your stuff."

"And what if I say no?" von Reich responded.

"There are other ways of putting you to sleep," said Joe. He bunched his fist in front of the doctor's face.

"You will never get out of here," the doctor threatened, rolling up his sleeve. "When I wake up, I will have the pleasure of finding you in my power again. And I assure you, Virus B is a far more interesting substance than this drug." A minute later, the doctor was lying unconscious on the floor.

"He'll be out long enough for us to reach Peterson and get help. Let's go," said Joe. Then he saw his father still hadn't moved. "What's wrong, Dad?"

But before Fenton Hardy could answer, Joe heard another sound—the sound of the doorknob turning.

Here we go again, thought Joe. He flattened himself against the wall on one side of the doorway, while Frank did the same on the other side.

The door swung open.

Joe and Frank tensed to spring.

Then, without warning, the script changed.

"Don't come in—my boys are waiting for you!" Fenton Hardy shouted.

And everything froze.

Joe and Frank couldn't do anything. They felt paralyzed.

All they could think was that their own father had betrayed them!

Chapter

13

"OKAY, FILE OUT of the room with your hands up," said Trask's bodyguard. He had been alerted by Fenton Hardy's warning shout. In the man's hand was an ugly-looking Uzi. But the look on his face was even uglier than the gun.

"Do what he says. Don't even think of getting the best of him," Fenton Hardy advised his sons, his eyes swimming with worry.

"No talk—just move it," the bodyguard snarled. He'd glanced into the lab and seen the doctor lying out cold on the floor. "I wouldn't want to be in your shoes once the boss finds out what you did to the doctor."

Trask's face flushed with rage when he heard the news. "Wise guy, huh?" he said to Hardy.

"You forgot what I told you. I got a good mind to pull the plug on those dames of yours."

"But it was the kids who did it, and they didn't know," protested Mr. Hardy.

"That's what you say," sneered Trask.

Desperation flooded the boys' father's voice. "Please. Believe me. You don't think they'd have tried anything if they knew."

"Knew *what?*" asked Joe.

"Quiet!" ordered Trask, whirling to face him. Then he turned back to face Fenton Hardy.

"Okay, I'll let it go this time," Trask said reluctantly. "But tell your kids the score. From now on no more excuses."

Mr. Hardy turned to his sons. "Sorry for fouling up your plans—but I had no choice. Trask's men have taken your mother and your aunt prisoner in Bayport. All Trask has to do is make a phone call, and Gertrude and your mother are dead."

"Dad, he's conning you," said Joe.

"Right," said Frank. "It's Mom and Aunt Gertrude who have the prisoners. We left them at home holding the goons at gunpoint."

Trask gave out a hoarse laugh. "You really think a couple of women could keep my men under their thumbs? Your luck ran out. The situation in Bayport is reversed, and your mother and aunt are paying for it."

"You're lying!" said Joe.

But the cold contempt in Trask's voice chilled

him. "Want to bet on it? Want to bet your mother's and aunt's lives?"

"You see why I had to stop you," Fenton Hardy said. "If we tried to escape, it wouldn't be just our lives we were putting on the line. And how could we really have been certain that Trask wouldn't have released Virus B in the meantime and wiped out the city? No," Mr. Hardy said thoughtfully, "the risk was too great."

Frank and Joe nodded. They should have known their dad had a good reason for doing what he did. They just hoped he could come up with something to get them out of this jam.

The brothers glanced at their father's face but couldn't see a glimmer of hope. He, like them, was alert, but the tight line of Fenton Hardy's mouth told his sons that he, too, couldn't see an escape. Time was running out for them all.

Thinking about time made Frank ask suddenly, "Hey, Trask, how long were we knocked out? What's been going on?"

"You weren't out long enough," Trask said.

"Long enough for what?" asked Frank. "Long enough for you to get videos of us to send to Peterson?" he guessed.

"That's it on the nose, kid," said Trask. "I told Peterson that if he didn't put his hands on the ransom real fast, all the males in the Hardy family would get it." Trask glanced at his watch. "Hey, you know what?"

Finally Joe gave in. "Okay, Trask, I'll bite. What?" he asked.

"The time I gave Peterson—it was up five minutes ago. Let's see how much that cop thinks your lives are worth."

Trask picked up his phone and punched out a number.

"Was the dough delivered?" he asked.

His face darkened as he heard the answer. He slammed down the receiver.

"Nothing yet. Not a cent," he growled. "All Peterson left at the drop-off point was a note begging for more time. Seems the big-money boys want proof of what kind of danger they're in."

Trask crashed his big fist down on his desk. The desk trembled. Trask was in his fifties, but the huge muscles in his arms were those of a younger man.

"I'll give them all the proof they want," he said, glaring at the Hardys. A nasty smile shaped his thick lips. "You think three Hardy corpses should do it?" He faced Fenton Hardy. "What do *you* think, Mr. Big Important Man?"

Before he could answer, Trask changed course. "Nah. A two-bit private eye and two baby boys wouldn't be impressive enough to make those fat cats cough up that big a chunk of their loot. Besides, Fenton, old buddy, I don't want you to die just yet. I want you around—that way you can see what kind of guy you were dealing with when you tangled with me."

Trask nodded at his bodyguard. "Come on. We're all going to the lab. Keep your guns on these jokers. You can never tell what they'll come up with."

"Gonna check on how the doctor is?" the bodyguard asked his boss.

"As far as I'm concerned, that creep can stay out for good," said Trask. "In fact, he's better off if he does. It'll spare him the shock of finding out that his share of the take ain't going to be what he expected."

"Double-crossing your own partner," said Joe. "You're a real sweet guy."

Trask wasn't insulted. If anything, he looked as if he had received a compliment. "In this business, kid, nice guys finish last. Dead last."

In the lab, Trask poked the doctor with his toe. Von Reich groaned, then stirred.

A cloud passed over Trask's face. "That drug of his ain't so good," he muttered. He bent down and picked up the hypodermic that had fallen to the floor when the doctor had passed out. Trask's face brightened. "Hey, Doc only injected himself with a little bit of it. I always knew the man was shrewd."

By then von Reich's eyelids were fluttering open. He was struggling to sit up.

But a minute later he was back on the floor, totally unconscious. With a big smile, Trask had emptied the rest of the needle into his arm.

Trask went to the lab refrigerator and took out a tightly corked test tube. A row of identical test tubes remained there.

"Nice supply, huh?" Trask said, making sure the Hardys got a good view. "Enough to wipe out a whole city."

"I can't believe it was right there," said Frank, hitting his forehead with the palm of his hand.

Trask closed the refrigerator door, then, eyeing the test tube, he faked a toss to Joe.

He chuckled as Joe instinctively made a desperate grab at thin air. "Think I'd trust you to catch this, kid?" Trask sneered. "You drop it, and we're all dead in about three minutes. A real ugly way to go, too. You should have seen how the doc's lab rats writhed around before they croaked. Ugly sight, believe me. Real ugly.

"Tell you what," he said. He was clearly enjoying himself. "I'll let you carry the stuff."

He handed the test tube to Joe. Joe held it carefully as he looked at it. The test tube was filled with a clear liquid. Joe tried to remember what he had learned about viruses in biology. It was hard to imagine that the liquid in that test tube was the breeding ground for millions of organisms that only the most high-powered high-tech microscopes could identify.

"Unbelievable," he said.

"Gives you the creeps, huh?" said Trask. "Don't worry. You won't have to carry it far. Come on."

Once again they walked down the corridor. This time they headed past Trask's office, not stopping until they reached a metal ladder. Trask climbed up the ladder. He gave five sharp raps on the trapdoor just above his head. Then he paused before rapping three times more. When the door was lifted, Trask squeezed through what, for him was a narrow opening.

"Okay, the rest of you come up," he called down. "And, you Hardys, no funny business."

While Trask's bodyguard held a gun on them from below, the Hardys climbed the ladder. Joe was extra careful because of his deadly cargo. They reached a dimly lit basement and discovered Trask standing next to a man dressed in a janitor's outfit.

"Give him the test tube," said Trask. Joe obeyed.

"Be careful of this stuff," Trask told the man. "Insert it the way we planned. Then clear out fast."

The man made a face. "You don't have to tell me that," he said, already fiddling with a series of pipes. "I saw what happened to those mice. No way I'm going to let that happen to me."

"Now we go back to my office and wait," said Trask, taking one last look at what his man was doing.

"Wait for what?" asked Frank. He dreaded the answer.

"Wait for my man here to hook up the test tube to a timing device he's planted inside the building's central air-conditioning system. The device will smash the test tube open in five minutes." Trask wore a sinister smile. "After that happens," he said, "it should take about half an hour for the radio and TV people to report the tragedy. Maybe we'll hear even sooner."

"What makes you think the story will get on the news so fast?" asked Joe. "It's Sunday, no one's around."

"Hey, bright boy, I forgot to tell you what building my office is under," Trask said, gloating.

"Some kind of courthouse, right?" Joe asked.

"Wrong," Trask said, grinning. "We're standing directly under City Hall. Just think," he went on. "Peterson is having a special meeting with the mayor and the city council, trying to convince them that we're for real. Sunday or not, they're all there."

A horrifying picture suddenly appeared in all of the Hardys' minds.

"In a few minutes, they'll know they were wrong to doubt me—*dead* wrong."

Chapter

14

BACK IN HIS office, Trask sat down at his desk, leaned back in his chair, and turned on his TV. By then four of his hoods had come in. The atmosphere was that of a big party. The thugs sat drinking beer as they watched a silent image on the TV screen. In no time, they knew, the program would be interrupted by some grim-faced announcer. Then the sound would be turned up again as they got all the gruesome details. Meanwhile, Trask had plenty to say to fill the silence.

"That twenty million is practically in my pocket," he said, licking beer foam off his lips. "The fat cats will fall all over themselves to pay it when they see what's happened to their mayor and chief of police. After that, I can start getting even with my 'pals.' When I got out of the joint, I found out what kind of pals they were—they'd divided up all my territory. 'Tough luck,' they told me. I was out in the cold."

"Gee, rough break," said Joe sarcastically. "You can't trust anybody anymore."

"So that's why you had to move underground," said Frank. "It was the only area in the city still open to you."

"You got the picture," Trask said bitterly. He grimaced at the memory. "Well, in just a couple of minutes now, nobody's ever going to get the better of Nick Trask again," he said, smiling.

But after a couple of minutes of watching the silent TV screen, Trask was no longer smiling. The same nature show was continuing. Trask got up and switched channels. Everything was normal, on all the stations. He snapped off the set suddenly and snapped on a transistor radio, turning to an all-news station. The announcer was enthusiastically reporting the score of a Yankees game.

Grabbing his phone then, Trask punched out a number. He shouted into the mouthpiece, "What's going on? Why didn't the thing go off?" Pause. "Well, go find out!"

Trask threw down the receiver. It hit the floor, carrying the rest of the phone with it. Picking up the jumble of plastic and cord, Trask shook his head in disgust. "Can you believe it? That jerk was just sitting around having a beer. He didn't bother checking to see what was happening. No wonder he wound up in the joint."

The phone rang, and Trask snatched it up. "You sap," he exploded into the receiver after listening a minute. "You must've fouled up the timer. Get down to the basement and check it out!"

Again Trask slammed down the phone. "The meeting is still going on at City Hall. They all should've croaked by now, like those rats or mice or whatever von Reich used in his experiments."

Trask lit a cigarette. Then he noticed one was already burning on the edge of his ashtray. Stubbing both of them out, he stood up and started pacing.

"Getting a little nervous, are you?" Joe couldn't resist asking.

Trask was opening his mouth to snarl an answer when the phone rang again. He dashed for it and picked it up. "Yeah? What did you find?" he asked anxiously. His ear was plastered against the receiver. *"What!"* he exclaimed. "Are you kidding me?"

He listened a moment, then let the receiver drop. His eyes had a dazed expression.

"What happened?" Fenton Hardy asked.

"I don't get it," Trask muttered. "My man went down to the basement. The test tube was smashed, just the way we planned it. The air-conditioning system was working great." Trask's voice rose to a bellow of rage. *"Then what went wrong? No one's dead!"*

Trask shook his head in disbelief. "The guy must've made a mistake. I'll tell him to check it all out again."

He picked up the phone. After furiously punching out numbers, he stood openmouthed, waiting.

"Now *this* thing is on the fritz," he said savagely, storming out of the room. Almost as an afterthought, he called over his shoulder, "Come on, all of you. We're going to the lab. The doctor has a lot of explaining to do."

The Hardys were herded out of the room, and everyone followed Trask's trail.

Frank managed to whisper to Joe and his dad as they left the room, "For the time being, there's no way Trask can make a phone call."

The two nodded. They all knew what that meant. With the phone out, Trask couldn't order their mom and aunt killed. A chance to escape had just appeared—if they moved fast enough.

The trouble was, bullets moved faster. Three Uzis were trained on the Hardys, and the men holding them looked trigger happy.

When they reached the lab, Trask gave the bodyguard a nod, and the man took the key from his pocket and unlocked the door.

The Hardys glanced knowingly at each other. All three of them saw the bodyguard leave the key in the lock. When Trask led everyone into the lab, the door was left open.

Another aid to help them escape.

But the guns were still trained on them.

Trask went to the doctor, picked him up, and shook him like a rag doll.

Von Reich stayed out like a light.

"The doctor's drug worked okay," growled Trask. "So what went wrong with his virus? He swore it worked. 'A hundred percent effective,' he said."

Letting the doctor drop to the floor, Trask glared down at the unconscious body. He looked as if he wanted to kick it. In fact, his foot actually was poised to deliver a kick when, instead, he turned away.

Having second thoughts, he turned back. Joe and Frank winced as they witnessed him deliver a vicious kick to the doctor's side. What if Trask's rage turned against *them?*

But Trask had a more pressing concern.

"Let's see if the doctor has anything to hide," he said slyly. "Some cute little secrets. The guy insisted on living in this lab. Claimed he wanted to be close to his work. But maybe he stayed here because he didn't want to leave his personal stuff unprotected. Maybe he had something he didn't want anyone to find."

Trask stormed over to a corner of the lab where a bed and a chest of drawers were set up. First he attacked the chest of drawers. His methods were crude but effective. He simply pulled out one drawer after another and dumped their contents on the floor.

All he found, though, were shirts, underwear, and socks.

By then three of Trask's men had joined him in rummaging around the doctor's living space. The remaining two kept their Uzis on the Hardys. The three prisoners were feeling restless.

"Looks like the doctor kept his bag packed," said one of the men. "Maybe he figured he'd have to clear out in a hurry."

He pulled a leather suitcase out from under the doctor's bed.

"Let's take a look," said Trask. He tried to open the suitcase, but it was locked. Shrugging, he pulled out a .45 automatic. The sound of the shot was deafening. Rows of empty test tubes on the walls trembled. But Trask wasn't interested. Not after he'd shoved aside the shattered lock and taken a look inside the suitcase.

"Dough!" he said, nearly pop-eyed. And at the sound of that magic word, his men gathered around him to stare at the contents.

"*My* dough," said Trask. "All the dough I gave the doctor for his 'experiments.' I should have known better than to trust a guy who was sent up for selling a phony cure for cancer. The rat was pulling a scam on me. Those test tubes must've been filled with a hundred percent water. He must have dosed his lab animals with poison to make me think Virus B was working. The double-crosser was going to take the money and run."

His face twisted with rage, Trask reached for his gun and swung around. He glowered at the prone body of the doctor. His men, though, were far more fascinated by the stacks of neatly bundled currency in the suitcase. They stared at them as if hypnotized.

Joe, Frank, and Fenton Hardy, though, didn't care about the money. They were more interested in the two guards who still had guns on them.

And in the open bottles of liquid that Joe and Frank only had to reach out to grab off the lab table.

They reached. They grabbed.

I hope this stuff is strong, Frank prayed silently as he flung the liquid in the nearest guard's face. His brother's bottle followed quickly, splashing in the face of the second guard.

The men's agonized screams gave the boys their answer.

By that time all three Hardys were through the doorway. Fenton Hardy slammed the lab door and turned the key in the lock. "Move fast," he said, "before Trask can get to a phone and contact the men holding your mom and aunt. As soon as we're clear, we can alert the Bayport police."

The Hardy boys needed no urging. In fact, they had to keep their speed down so their dad could keep up with them.

"We'll be out of here in no time," exulted Joe as they dashed down a corridor and whipped around a corner.

"Not quite," said Frank. As they made the turn, they almost fell over their own feet braking to a stop.

Coming toward them were four men, all brandishing pistols.

"The other way!" ordered Fenton Hardy, and the three raced back around the corner and down the corridor.

But they hadn't made it halfway to the lab when they heard the rapid firing of an Uzi. The lab door flew open, its shattered lock clattering to the floor. Trask and his men poured out, guns drawn.

The Hardys wheeled around again, but the four gunmen who had cut off their escape were turning the corner and sighting in on them.

Spinning one last time, the Hardys came face to face with Trask's fury. On either side of him, his hired guns were swinging up to take dead aim.

"Uh-oh," said Joe.

"We're trapped," said Frank.

But their dad summed it up best.

"We're dead."

Chapter

15

FENTON HARDY HAD another word of wisdom for his sons. It was based on years of experience.

"Dive!" he said.

Frank and Joe were already ahead of him. As their father did, they knew that guns tended to jerk upward when fired. Diving, they might avoid the first rounds coming at them. After that, though, they would be done for.

But lying flat on the floor, they heard bullets continue to whiz over their heads. What was happening? Trask's thugs couldn't shoot that badly.

Then the shooting stopped. The Hardys looked up and saw that the men who had cut off their escape were gone.

"Get up, before I leave you lying there—permanently," Trask said, frowning down at them.

From their vantage point, they were looking straight into the barrel of his gun. His men stood behind him, their Uzis smoking.

"Come on, on your feet," Trask said. "And no more funny business. You Hardys are lucky I still need you alive."

Back in the lab, he told them, "So now you see what kind of friends my old pals are. I got a little short and had to borrow from them, and then, just because I got a bit behind in my payments, they send in muscle to collect. As if they couldn't trust me to make good on a lousy couple hundred grand."

"An honest guy like you," said Joe with mock sympathy.

"Kid, someday you're going to open your mouth too wide and find a gun rammed down your throat," Trask spat out. Then he said, "But I have more important things to do right now. Like get uptown to Grand Central. We can contact Peterson from there. We still have a chance to put the squeeze on the city for the dough. They don't know it's a bluff yet—and they'll pay rather than risk it."

Trask turned to his men. "Come on, you guys. And keep the Hardys covered. If they even look like they're making a break, don't ask questions. Blow them away."

Trask started for the door, the suitcase full of

money in one hand, his gun in the other. Then he stopped. None of his men had made a move.

"Come on," he snapped. "I said let's go."

"You didn't tell us we'd be in a war against the mob," the bodyguard complained, and the other four nodded. "That wasn't part of the deal."

"And we ain't been paid in three weeks," said one of the others. "That wasn't part of the deal either."

"So you can count us out," said another one.

"And we'll take the dough in the suitcase to cover what you owe us," said the third.

"Hand it over," said the fourth.

Instinctively, Trask started to raise his gun. Then, taking a look at the Uzis trained on him, he thought better of it and tossed the suitcase at the feet of his bodyguard.

"Here," he snarled. "Take it. And good luck. You'll need it."

The bodyguard grabbed the suitcase. He and the others were out of the room in a flash. They left the door open behind them, and their running footsteps could be heard heading down the corridor.

"Those morons don't have enough brains to figure out that the organization has this place surrounded," Trask said. "Just like they cut off my phones so I couldn't call for help from uptown. Those jerks don't have a chance of getting out of here."

"And you do?" asked Frank.

"You bet I do—and I'm taking you with me," said Trask. He motioned with his gun for the Hardys to move out of the room ahead of him. "I'm not beaten yet."

"Just hold on a minute," Fenton Hardy boomed. His voice stopped Trask cold. "Have you thought about this—with that old man Ian dead, you're up against a murder rap. The best thing for you would be to turn yourself in."

"But that guy didn't die from the virus—there was no virus."

Fenton Hardy scowled. "You think the police will care about that?"

Trask considered Hardy's words. Then a crooked smile erupted on his face. "Well, my dear friend," he said, sneering, "if I'm going to be sent up for killing *one* guy"—Trask's gaze swept over the three—"then I might as well kill three more!"

Ten minutes later, after moving through a maze of corridors, tunnels, and an old water main, the group emerged into a subway station—or what was once a subway station. By then Trask had taken a flashlight out of his pocket. In its beam the Hardys could see elaborate tilework that was now cracked and covered with grime.

"This used to be the City Hall station," said Trask. "A real fancy place once, from what they tell me. What you call a showcase. But the station's been deserted for years."

"What do we do now, catch the phantom express?" asked Frank, looking around. He felt strange standing there, as if he were in a haunted house.

"Shut up and listen," said Trask. "Fenton, get closer to me. I'm going to be carrying my gun in my jacket pocket, and it's going to be pointed right at you. So if your kids get any ideas of making a break for it, you're going to pay."

Just then a roaring filled the station as a train went by.

"We're going down on the tracks," Trask said when he could be heard again. "We can make it to the next stop before another train comes."

Five minutes later, people waiting on the next subway platform saw four figures—two mature men and two teens—emerging from the darkness of the tunnel and climbing up onto the platform.

"Some people will do anything to beat the fare," one woman said to her companion. But as far as the Hardys could make out, everyone else looked the other way.

Ten minutes after that, the next train finally arrived. The commuters jammed into the already packed cars. Trask stayed close to Fenton Hardy, who felt Trask's pistol poking into his back. Afraid for their father, Frank and Joe made no move to escape.

After several stops, the train made it to Grand Central.

Fenton Hardy felt Trask's gun give him a painful jab, and he and his sons moved in front of the hoodlum and off the train.

"We're home free," said Trask, and fifteen minutes later they were underground again, in another of Trask's headquarters.

"It's practically payday now," Trask assured the six men he had gathered in the room. His voice was full of hearty good cheer. "Just a couple of phone calls, and we're all rich."

"About time," muttered one of the men.

Trask's tone changed abruptly. "One more wisecrack, and you're out in the cold. Got it?"

"Just kidding," the man apologized.

"You better be," growled Trask.

"That you, Peterson?" Trask snarled after reaching for the phone and punching out a number. "I hope by now you've given up trying to trace my calls. Now listen and listen hard. I want that dough you promised me and I want it fast. Don't jerk me around, Mr. Almost Mayor. It won't do much for your campaign if I kill the Hardys—yeah, *all* of them—and then I start on the rest of the city. You didn't know I had the Hardy kids along with their dad? Here. Pay attention."

He handed the phone to Frank. "Tell him the good news, kid."

"Peterson?" Frank said into the receiver. The chief sounded hoarse to him. He had the voice of a man who had been talking too much and not getting enough sleep.

"Yes, he's got us," Frank went on when Peterson asked him to confirm.

Trask took the phone back. "Convinced?" He smiled. "Good. Now, like I said, I want the money fast.

"What do you mean, you have just five million?" Trask said. He'd been listening to Peterson's reply. "What am I supposed to do with chicken feed like that? It'll barely cover expenses." Trask concentrated. "Okay," he said. "I'll agree to that. You leave the five million at the drop-off point as agreed and get me the rest in two days. You've bought that much time—but, Peterson"—Trask looked at the Hardys—"you cross me, you even make me *think* you're crossing me, and your friends are dead meat."

Trask wore a triumphant expression as he put the phone down. "I knew they'd chicken out. They don't have enough guts to see a few lousy lives lost. That's why tough guys like me always come out on top."

"You're on the bottom as far as I'm concerned," Joe said, and Trask shoved him hard.

Then the hood turned to his men and told two of them to pick up the parcel at the drop-off point. "It should be there in ten minutes," he said. "Keep your eyes peeled so you're not followed. I don't figure Peterson's going to pull a fast one.

Still, you can't be sure. He must be getting a lot of heat from the fat cats. They ain't into giving away their dough."

After the men left, Trask gave the rest of his crew a little pep talk. "Boys, you've done good work for me, and when Nick Trask gets good work, he pays good for it. You know the dough I told you you'd get when this job was finished? Well, I'm going to double it, just as soon as that final payment is made. Plus all of you are going to have executive jobs in the organization I'm setting up. You'll be kings of the city, and I don't mean the underground. We'll be moving up in the world soon, taking over everything."

It took just twenty minutes for Trask's messengers to return with a satchel.

"Let me see that," Trask said, reaching out for it.

He turned all his attention to the satchel. Putting it on his desk, he started unloading the contents—bundle after bundle of hundred-dollar bills. He counted the bills in the first bundle, then used that stack to measure the thickness of all the other bundles he took out. After counting the total number, he did a quick multiplication on a small calculator and announced, "Five million on the nose."

But he wasn't quite finished. He took a magnifying glass from the desk drawer. Examining two bills closely, he gave a final nod. "Good," he said. "Peterson didn't mark them. Guess he knows that Nick Trask is no chump."

Trask then began to load the bundles back into the satchel, casually sweeping the two loose bills onto the floor.

When one of his men bent to pick them up, Trask said, "Don't bother, that's small stuff. In two days you're going to have more dough than you can stuff in your pockets."

The thug hesitated. Then, giving the bills a quick glance, he backed off from them.

"You guys are in the big time now," Trask told them. "You've got to learn to think big. But, of course, we still have to keep on our toes. That's why I'm sending you out to make sure the cops don't try to find this place. You already know your guardposts, so get to them fast. Make sure nobody sneaks by you."

Trask waited until the last of his men had left. Then, with his gun covering the Hardys, he went to the door and locked it. Next he bent over, picked up the hundred-dollar bills he had grandly swept to the floor, and stuck them into his wallet.

"Never know when a couple of hundred will come in handy," he said, "though I won't really need them. Not with the rest of this pile here."

Moving to the satchel stuffed with money, he snapped it closed. Then he picked it up, testing its weight.

"Not as heavy as I thought," he said. "I'll be able to make good time with it."

The Hardys looked at one another.

"Are you thinking what I'm thinking?" Frank asked his dad.

"The thought crossed my mind," he answered.

"What are you two talking . . . oh, I see what you mean," Joe said. He shook his head at Trask. "Hey, Nick, I'm surprised at you. You wouldn't be thinking of stealing that five mil, would you?"

Trask's grin grew even wider. "You Hardys are smart, aren't you? Sure, I'm getting out while the getting is good and the coast is clear. Five mil will do me just fine."

"If there's one thing I've learned in this case," said Joe, smiling ruefully, "it's never to believe that stuff you hear about honor among thieves. Crooks are crooks, and that's it."

"Hey, I'm glad you wised up," said Trask. "It's a real shame you won't be able to use what you've learned. The problem is, all you Hardys know too much, and you just can't stay alive."

He leveled his gun at Joe, Frank, and Fenton Hardy, making a sweeping motion in front of their faces.

"Okay, let's not waste time," he said. "Which one of you wants to get it first?"

Chapter

16

THE HARDYS LOOKED at one another, each hoping the others would see a way out. But all they saw were helpless expressions.

"Hey, don't look so down in the dumps. I'm being a nice guy," Trask mocked. "I'm letting you choose what order you want to die in. So don't waste my time, or I'll let my gun do the deciding."

Before Frank or Joe could make a move, their dad stepped forward. He was shielding them now and looking up at Trask.

"Hey, that's nice, Fenton, real nice," said Trask. "You've lived a lot longer than your kids, so now you're going to give *them* some extra time. I'm sure they'll appreciate it for the rest of their lives—all one minute more."

Then Trask paused, as if having second thoughts. "But maybe I shouldn't waste you first. I mean, it might be fun making you watch your own two kids get it."

But Trask didn't have the pleasure of watching Fenton Hardy plead or squirm. He stood in front of Trask without wavering, his gaze level and hard. Finally, Trask shrugged, tiring of his game. "Okay, Fenton, I'll be Mr. Nice Guy. You get it first, and you can just think of what your kids will feel like when they watch you go."

Trask extended his arm. He aimed directly at the center of Fenton Hardy's forehead. At a distance of less than four feet, there wasn't a chance in the world of his missing the target.

Hardy, lips drawn tight, stared into the gun barrel without flinching.

Frank and Joe felt sick to their stomachs. They couldn't bear to watch what was going to happen, yet they couldn't tear their eyes away from their last look at their dad.

Trask's eyes shone happily. "I won't say it's been nice knowing you, Fenton. But it's sure going to be nice killing—"

To Frank and Joe, braced for horror, the sound of the phone ringing was louder than a pistol shot.

Trask was startled as well. His gun hand held steady, but his face swiveled around to look at the ringing phone.

That was all Fenton Hardy needed. He lunged

for Trask's gun, grabbing the barrel with both hands and using every ounce of his strength to wrench it from his iron grip.

But that still left Trask's other hand free—free enough to smash into Fenton Hardy's jaw. Still clutching the gun, he crashed backward against a wall, then collapsed in a heap.

Trask snickered loudly and went after Hardy, his hand out to snatch the gun back.

But before he could take two steps, Joe hit him around the knees in a perfect low tackle. Joe had brought down charging fullbacks with tackles just like it. But all he succeeded in doing then was stopping Trask's forward movement.

The guy's built like a brick wall, was the only thing Joe had time to think before Trask grabbed him and tore himself loose. Roaring, he pitched Joe against the wall.

Joe, half-stunned, desperately tried to clear his head. At the same time, he watched Frank deliver a perfect karate chop to Trask's upper arm. The chop looked as if it could have felled a tree, but all it did was make Trask grunt. Trask's other arm hooked around toward Frank in a vicious counterpunch that Frank barely dodged. But he couldn't duck Trask's kick. It caught him on an ankle and sent him sprawling.

"Hey, Nick baby, look at me!" Joe yelled just as Trask was raising his foot for another kick that would have laid Frank's head wide open.

But the crook did what Joe hoped he would—he hesitated and turned to face Joe. Joe butted him in the pit of the stomach with the top of his head, his legs pumping like pistons.

He *has* to go down now, Joe thought, hearing the *whoosh* of Trask's breath as it was knocked out of him. But he had hardly finished thinking that when he felt Trask's fist cracking against his jaw.

Joe saw stars. Through them he made out the phantom shape of Frank charging Trask once again. But Trask smashed Frank.

The Hardy boys were beside each other then, both of them reeling on the floor as Trask stood over them, grinning. The boys tried to move when Trask reached out to grab them, but their battered bodies weren't able to follow the commands of their clearing brains.

Then each of them was being lifted off the ground, Frank in Trask's left hand, Joe in his right. They heard Trask's voice, harsh with pain and rage. "You punk kids figure two heads are better than one, I bet. Let's see how good your two heads are when I smash them together."

Frank and Joe tried to struggle, but their bodies still would not obey.

All they could do was brace themselves for the violent agony they would feel when their skulls were smashed together. All they could do was ready themselves for the inevitable blackout.

But their luck held.

"Owwwwww!" howled Trask. Then his voice turned dull. "Ugh," he grunted.

Frank and Joe felt themselves released from his grip as, with a surprised look on his face and like a huge falling tree, Trask slowly toppled over.

Behind him Fenton Hardy stood with Trask's gun raised, ready to strike a third blow if necessary.

"I thought for a second he wasn't going to go down," Fenton said. "He's got a head like a rock. You kids okay? Good thing I came to in time."

"I've got nothing that a couple of aspirin won't cure," said Joe, rubbing his sore chin.

Frank looked down at Trask. "When he goes back to jail, they'd better not let him get at that bodybuilding equipment again."

"Hey, he didn't stand a chance," said Joe. "Not against us." He grinned at his dad. "All *three* of us."

Then the Hardys noticed something they'd put out of their consciousness during the fight. The phone was still ringing.

"Let's see how well I can imitate Trask's voice," Fenton Hardy said.

He picked up the receiver. "Yeah," he growled. "What do you want? And make it quick."

He listened for a minute. "What do they look like?" he rasped.

Another silence. The investigator hung up without saying goodbye.

"It was one of Trask's men," he said worriedly. "He said they were being attacked at all their guardposts. But before he could tell me who was doing the attacking, the line went dead."

"Maybe the cops got to them," said Joe.

"Doesn't seem likely," said Frank. "The guy would have said that right away."

"I've got a better idea," said their father. "The mob must have traced Trask up here. And now they're coming to get him."

"It figures," said Joe, nodding. "I bet they captured some of Trask's men downtown. It wouldn't have taken much to make them talk."

"The mob isn't coming just to get Trask," Frank thought out loud. "They're coming to get us too. No way they'll leave any live witnesses around."

"We have to get out of here fast," said his dad.

"And lug big boy here with us," said Joe, looking down at the unconscious Trask. "What a pain. Maybe we should just leave him here for his old pals to take care of."

"Forget it," said his dad. "We're working for the law, not the lawless."

"Just a thought," said Joe. "Come on, Frank, help me move man-mountain here."

He bent to grab Trask by one arm. Frank bent to grab the other, but the sound of someone trying to open the door made them both straighten up fast.

"Too late," their father said. "We're trapped."

He leveled the gun at the door. "The only thing we can do," he said, "is try to take as many of them with us as we can."

"Right, Dad," the boys said. But it occurred to them that what they really were saying was good-bye.

Chapter

17

AN AX SMASHED through the door around the lock.

The door swung open.

And Frank and Joe shouted at the top of their lungs, "Don't shoot!"

But they shouted their warning in opposite directions.

Frank shouted at his dad, who was standing facing the door with his gun leveled.

Joe shouted at the open doorway, where, gun in hand and in the same firing position, stood Peter Jones.

Both men lowered their guns, and both Hardy boys breathed a sigh of relief.

Jones stuck his gun into the belt of his seersucker suit. Over his shoulder, he said, "It's okay. We're among friends."

He entered the room followed by six men. All were carrying weapons. One of the men was a wiry Latino in a gray sweatsuit. The other five, three of them black, two white, all of them bearded and two with hair in ponytails, wore old army fatigues.

"Meet my strike force," Jones said after the Hardy boys introduced him and their dad to each other. "Carlos here was once a lightweight contender. And each of these vets makes Rambo look like a Boy Scout. Those crooks didn't know what hit them. We took the entire arsenal we're carrying from them. As soon as we lifted a gun from the first one we ambushed, the rest came easy."

"Lucky for us you decided to attack when you did," said Frank. "If that crook hadn't made that desperate phone call, we'd be lying there the way Trask is now. Except that we'd be dead."

"It wasn't luck—it was underground people power," said Jones proudly. "You probably didn't notice it, but there was an old woman nesting down in the old City Hall subway station. She saw Trask herding you onto the uptown tracks, and she figured it might have something to do with the struggle up here. So she gave us a call, and I got our act together."

"We'd better get *our* act together," Fenton

Hardy told his sons. "Your mom and Gertrude are still in danger. First thing we do is call the Bayport police and alert them to the situation. They can surround the house."

Fenton Hardy was smiling when he put down the receiver after talking to the police. "I should have known that a couple of crooks couldn't get the best of Laura. When they tried some funny business, she laid them out cold. Then she contacted Collig and had him lock them up—with the understanding, of course, that he'd keep the whole operation quiet until I told her my assignment was finished."

"So Trask was lying when he said his men were holding Mom and Aunt Gertrude captive," said Joe.

"Why so surprised?" asked Frank. "Ever since we went underground, nothing's been quite what it seemed. I've been feeling like I wandered into Alice's Wonderland."

"Yeah," said Joe. "This whole case was a great big web of lies—which reminds me," he added, "what *did* happen to Ian? How did he die?"

Jones's face went slack. "Heart attack," he said sadly. "The doctor's drug was too much for him. If he'd been stronger, Ian would be with us now, celebrating."

"Which *we* can do now, thank goodness," said Mr. Hardy. He picked up the phone again. "I can hardly wait to tell Sam Peterson the good news. This whole thing must have been like a nightmare for him."

But Peterson still had one last concern.

He explained it two hours later in a very private meeting in his office. He'd asked Fenton Hardy, Joe and Frank, and Peter Jones to stop by.

"When the media start asking questions," Peterson said after his secretary had left the room, "it's going to be hard to explain what happened. I mean, I appreciate the help that the underground people provided. But officially they're not even supposed to be living down there, much less doing the job of the police."

"Which wouldn't exactly help your image when you run for mayor, right, Chief?" said Peter Jones with a smile.

"That, too, of course," Peterson acknowledged.

"I think I have a way out of your dilemma," Jones said, his smile warm. "And out of a lot of other people's dilemmas as well."

"Oh? What's that?" asked Peterson with keen interest.

"I'd be glad to have my people provide eyewitness testimony to how the police made an underground raid at Grand Central and caught the Trask gang. The raid was astounding, they'll testify, its success hinging on the help of undercover

148

cops disguised as underground people. That should go a long way in making you a hero. It might also make you a mayor."

"And why would you do all that for me?" Peterson asked. His eyes narrowed slightly.

"I can see you've started thinking like a politician already," said Jones with a grin. "You're right. I do want something. I want a strong commitment from you. If you're elected mayor, I'd like you to be sympathetic to the city's homeless population. Some people prefer to live underground, but most of them are forced to. And I think it's the city's job to help bring these people into the light again. Do you agree to help us?"

"I agree," said Peterson. "And I also agree with what you said and want to help."

"Will you put it in writing?" asked Jones.

"I may sound like a politician, but you sound even more like a lawyer," the chief said, chuckling. "Sure, I'll put it in writing. In fact, I'll do even more than that to assure you I'll keep my word. How would you like a job in my administration if I'm elected? I'll need people like you around me—people who can keep me in touch with everyone in the city I'm supposed to serve."

"Chief," Jones promised, "you have yourself a new aide—and I think you're going to have a whole bunch of very effective new campaign workers."

Jones and Peterson shook hands firmly. The Hardys looked on.

"I guess we can be getting back to Bayport," Fenton Hardy said then. "We're leaving New York in pretty good hands."

"Before you go, you have to promise me something," Peterson said. "At least your kids have to."

"What's that?" asked Frank.

"In a few years, when you're considering jobs, think about joining the New York City Police Department," said Peterson. "You're the best prospects I've seen since the old days when your dad and I put on uniforms."

"Chips off the old block, Sam," Fenton Hardy agreed, placing a hand on each of his sons' shoulders. "Chips off the old block."

"Come on, we're a couple of high school kids," said Joe. "We just want to have fun. No more crime fighting for us."

And now it was the Hardy boys' turn to exchange great big grins.

Frank and Joe's next case:

Frank and Joe Hardy know that "Uncle" Hugh Hunt isn't really an uncle. He's an old friend of their father's—an insurance salesman, and to tell the truth, a bit of a bore.

So why would anyone feed him a slow-acting poison?

The Hardys have only three days to find out. And as they investigate, Frank and Joe find spies, thieves, and some things about Uncle Hugh that they never suspected.

They also discover the plans for a major jewel robbery. Will Frank and Joe be forced to break the law to save a life? Find out in *The Crowning Terror*, Case #6 in The Hardy Boys Casefiles.

The Hardy Boys Mystery Stories

ARMADA

The Three Investigators
Series

Meet the Three Investigators – brilliant Jupiter Jones, athletic Pete Crenshaw and studious Bob Andrews. Their motto, "We investigate anything" has led them into some bizarre and dangerous situations. Join the three boys in their sensational mysteries, available only in Armada.

ARMADA

SPY FILES

COULD YOU BECOME
A SPYCATCHER?

Tap phones . . . Trail suspects . . .
Decipher codes . . . Monitor key locations . . .
Consult the Secret Service computer

To solve each of the espionage crimes you must
piece together all the evidence taken from
individual case files and the information held on
the Secret Service computer. Only by skilful
intelligence work will you be able to catch the
spies. All the information is here – but like any
good counter-espionage agent, you have to be
logical and sharp-witted . . .

A game for one or more players.

£2.95 ☐

ARMADA